Ghost at the Ballet School

Cassie's ears were straining. She heard some faint rustling sounds. Then nothing. She waited. Again the rustling sounds.

She sat up in bed and stared at the door, willing herself to see through it. Whatever was making those sounds was right outside. She held her breath.

The brass doorknob rattled and slowly turned. The door eased open slightly. Cassie was wide-eyed. Her heart thumped in her chest.

A hand appeared in the gap. A white, slender hand, with long pale fingers, pointing, pointing straight at Cassie. . .

Further titles to come in the Ballet School *series*

1   Cassie at the Ballet School
2   Ghost at the Ballet School
3   New Friends at the Ballet School
4   Trouble at the Ballet School
5   On Tour with the Ballet School
6   Stars of the Ballet School

Ghost at the Ballet School

Mal Lewis Jones

**Hodder
Children's
Books**

A division of Hodder Headline plc

For my parents and the Lewis and Todd clans.

Contents

1	A Special Assembly	1
2	The Figure in White	13
3	Old Friends	25
4	A Ghostly Visitor	37
5	Red Riding Hood	47
6	Midnight Meeting	59
7	Chief Suspect	69
8	Sick-bay	83
9	Half-term Outings	95
10	Imprisoned	105
11	The Ghost Returns	119
12	Ghost at the Window	127
13	The Charm Bracelet	139
14	End of the Hunt	151

1

A Special Assembly

Cassie Brown took a deep breath and turned a perfect pirouette.

If only Madame Larette could have seen that one, she thought, gazing out of the window at the towering redwood trees in the grounds. The rhododendrons, early this year, bloomed a rich purple, while the sun sparkled on their glossy leaves. Her friend Becky Hastings was still sleeping, but the third bed in the small room, which was Amanda Renwick's, was already empty.

This was Cassie's third term at Redwood Ballet School and the first time she had felt thoroughly homesick. Her parents had worried about her going away to boarding school, when she had surprised them by winning a scholarship to Redwood. They had thought eleven far too young to go away from home, but as it turned out, Cassie had settled in quite happily to the new routine of ballet school life. She had made some very good friends and spending half lesson-time in dance class was like a dream come true.

Seeing her family every holiday and some weekends, she was still able to share everything with them. But now Cassie thought of her two-year-old sister, Rachel, and had a sudden longing to be there at home with her.

She hung her head as her mind went back to the previous day's test. How she had let herself down! Every single pirouette she had turned had ended in a wobble. Her pliés had been jerky and her grands battements at the barre had stayed sadly at half-mast.

But now the test was over, she could turn two pirouettes with ease. Ending the turns, facing the tall wardrobe mirror, she saw herself land in a perfect plié, knees beautifully turned out over toes, elbows rounded, hands gracefully composed. The high cheekbones and wide brow of her face gave extra depth to her brown, velvety eyes, as they stared back at her from the glass, framed prettily by her long, wavy brown hair.

'What's the matter?' asked Becky sleepily, as she sat up in bed.

'I could just kick myself for mucking up my pre-

2

exam test. I don't think Madame will let me take my Grade Five now!'

'Well, there's always next year. Don't worry about it,' said Becky, yawning.

Cassie sighed and thought what a happy-go-lucky nature her friend had. In other ways too, they made a striking contrast: Becky had the palest of blonde hair and very white skin and was shorter and stockier than Cassie.

'Aren't *you* bothered that you're not being put in for the exam?' Cassie asked.

'Course not,' Becky snorted. 'You know me. The less work the better.'

This wasn't entirely true. Cassie knew how hard her friend worked in Maths and Science.

'Sometimes I think you don't like being at ballet school at all,' Cassie said, shaking her head.

Becky shrugged. 'I enjoy being with you and Emily. We've had some great fun. But it was my mum who wanted me to come here in the first place.'

'Why's that?'

'Oh, she always wanted to be a dancer herself, but Gran and Grandad couldn't afford to send her to ballet school. So she wants to give me the chance she didn't have.' Becky grinned. 'Only trouble is, I don't want it!'

'Mmmm,' said Cassie. 'A bit tricky. But don't go off and leave me, for goodness sake. I'd be left on my own with Amanda!'

Just then Emily, their friend from the next room,

3

already dressed in the regulation red track suit, poked her head round the door.

Her normally pale face had acquired a crop of freckles from spending a sunny Easter holiday at home. A small, sensitive girl, almost bird-like in her movements, Emily had almost had to leave ballet school after the first term, because of her family's lack of money. Luckily, Emily had been awarded a bursary for her uniform and equipment.

'Hi!' she said brightly. 'Come on, you two! You'll be late for breakfast.'

Cassie, already wearing her pink leotard, pulled on her track suit and sat in front of the mirror to plait and pin up her hair, while Becky went off to the bathroom.

'Where's Amanda?' asked Emily.

'Guess.'

'Practising?'

'Got it in one. That girl never stops. But listen, Emily, have you noticed how friendly she's getting with Sharon and Sandra?'

'Yes, it's odd, isn't it,' said Emily. 'I mean, she knows they're both going to leave at the end of term, so why bother making friends with them? Amanda's never bothered with anyone much till now.'

Cassie shuddered. 'It must be absolutely terrible for the ones who've been told they have to leave in July. I don't think I could have faced coming back this term if I were them.'

'Like Miranda,' added Emily. 'I hate looking at

4

her empty bed in our room.'

During the Easter holidays, six girls had received letters from Miss Wrench containing the dreaded words: 'We regret we can no longer offer you a place at Redwood for the forthcoming academic year.'

Four of these unlucky ones, including Miranda, Emily's room-mate, had felt unable to come back for the summer term. Only Sharon and Sandra had returned, and the other girls had found it very difficult to know what to say to them.

The door burst open, nearly knocking Emily over. 'Watch out!' she cried, as Amanda Renwick flounced past, followed at a more leisurely pace by Becky, still in her nightdress. Amanda was wearing the purple designer-label outfit in which she had been doing her early morning practice and which, she had been at pains to tell everyone, had cost over a hundred pounds. The rich colour set off her olive skin and glossy black hair to perfection.

'Sorry,' she said sweetly.

She stretched out on the rug like a sleek cat and then pointed one foot towards the ceiling.

'Guess what,' she said, admiring the arch of her foot, 'Daddy's promised me a present if Madame enters me for Grade Five.'

Amanda lowered her leg and smiled innocently at Cassie. 'And she's just told me she's putting me in for it.'

Cassie went pale. Madame Larette had certainly not told *her* the same good news. And it was just like Amanda to come and gloat. She always seemed to do everything possible to irritate Cassie.

This term she seemed even more boastful than last. Cassie had tried hard to get on with her, especially as she was a room-mate, but she was finding it more and more difficult.

It had become clear to everyone that Amanda was Miss Wrench's star pupil and Cassie found this quite hard to cope with. She knew in her heart that she was every bit as talented as Amanda, although perhaps not so technically able.

'Looks like you'll be staying in Grade Five with Becky,' said Amanda.

'Oh shut up, Amanda,' snapped Cassie. 'Why don't you go and do some more practice.'

Amanda rose gracefully and began changing into her pink leotard, ready for ballet class. 'Well perhaps if you did a bit more work, you might be taking your exam.'

There was enough truth in this to sting Cassie into fury. She sprang to her feet wildly.

'Get lost,' she shouted. 'You think you're so wonderful, don't you!'

At this moment there was a knock on the door.

Emily answered it, and was surprised to find Miss Eiseldown standing there.

'Keep your voices down girls,' said the housemother sharply.

Cassie gulped down her words. Miss Eiseldown was a very understanding teacher, but did not like disturbances on her landing.

'Would you all come to the assembly hall

immediately, please? There's a special assembly.'

'What for?' chorused the four girls from the doorway.

'You'll find out soon enough,' said Miss Eiseldown, rather edgily. 'Come down as quickly as you can.'

Amanda stayed behind to put on her track suit, while Cassie, Becky and Emily joined the other girls from the landing making their way downstairs.

'It can't be a fire-drill,' said Becky. 'There's been no bell.'

'Perhaps Miss Wrench thinks we need some extra hymn practice,' joked Cassie, even though she felt quite anxious.

'It's bound to be something awful,' said Emily.

'Yes,' agreed Becky. 'They haven't even let us have breakfast first.'

Once the Juniors and Seniors who made up the Lower School had joined the residential staff in the assembly hall, and all fifty members of the Upper School had crammed themselves in behind them, Miss Wrench strode across to the rostrum, behind which two enormous stained glass windows shimmered in the light of early morning. She turned to the assembled students, the imposing gilt school crest just above her head.

'I have a very unpleasant announcement to make,' she began, sweeping the oak-panelled hall with her piercing green eyes. Her thin features, always accentuated by her hair drawn back into a tight, steel-grey bun, seemed sharper than ever.

7

'There has been a serious theft. The bronze cast of the ballet shoe of our revered Dame Anna Petrakova has been stolen from its glass case in the entrance hall.

'And what is worse, the police are sure that the thief–' Here she glanced along the rows of upturned faces, '–is a member of our school.'

A shocked murmur went round the hall, until it was quelled by a look from the green eyes.

Cassie thought back to her first visit to Redwood and how, as she had entered the main door with her parents, she had been thrilled by the sight which met her eyes: a full-length portrait of Petrakova in the long, white dress that the spirit of Giselle wears in the second act of the ballet. And, underneath that, a case displaying the shapely bronze cast of the great dancer's ballet shoe.

'I need hardly remind you,' went on Miss Wrench, 'that Dame Anna was our most famous pupil and her gift was highly valued. This theft is an *outrage!*'

Cassie and Emily both shivered at the note in their Principal's voice.

'The senseless individual who took it will be found!' warned Miss Wrench. 'And it would be better for him or her to own up *now*.' She paused dramatically, as if expecting someone to speak. 'Otherwise, the shadow of suspicion falls on every last one of you!'

With that, she swept from the hall back to her office. The children were dismissed and allowed to take a late breakfast. They were all at a fever pitch of excitement. Everyone had their own theory about how the ballet shoe had been stolen.

'What makes the police say it's an inside job?' asked Becky.

'I heard someone say the glass hadn't been smashed,' said Emily, who always had an ear to the ground for gossip.

'That's strange,' said Cassie. 'It means the right key must have been used to open the cabinet.'

'Unless the lock was picked,' suggested Becky.

Cassie had been thinking. 'There couldn't have been any sign of forced entry either,' she added, 'or the police wouldn't have ruled out a break-in.'

'Or perhaps someone just sneaked in before the caretaker locked up in the evening,' said Emily.

'Yes,' said Becky, warming to the idea, 'and hid somewhere till everyone was asleep.'

'But then how did he – or she – get out again?' asked Emily.

'And we come back to the business of the cabinet not being broken,' said Cassie. 'No, I think the police are right. It's someone at Redwood.'

But why should one of the children or teachers have stolen the shoe? It was very puzzling. The girls decided it was probably a prank thought up by one or two of the wilder senior boys, and that the bronze shoe would probably be quietly replaced – perhaps that very night.

'Shall we sneak a look before ballet class?' said Cassie excitedly.

'Great idea,' Becky agreed.

9

'I can't come,' said Emily. 'I've promised to help Jane with her History homework. See you later.'

Becky and Cassie weren't the only ones who were 'just passing through' the entrance hall and having a good look at the empty case.

Cassie gazed up at the expressive, painted face of Petrakova and sighed. To become a great dancer like her was the dream of so many young hopefuls at the Ballet School. Cassie couldn't imagine wanting to be anything else.

Becky brought her back to earth. 'Oh!' she exclaimed. 'I've dropped my hair-band. Did you see where it went?'

Cassie and Becky hunted round for it, but without success.

'It may have rolled under the cabinet,' Cassie suggested. Becky bent down and felt underneath.

'Oh yes, it's here,' she said. 'But there's something else as well!' She pulled out a tiny, silver ballerina.

'Let's see!' cried Cassie. 'Oh! Isn't it lovely? Someone must have lost it from a charm bracelet.'

'We'd better hand it in at the office,' said Becky.

'Shh!' hissed Cassie urgently. 'Stand up quick. The Wrench is coming.'

Becky automatically obeyed, just as Miss Wrench approached them.

'Don't loiter here!' she ordered. 'Go and get ready for class immediately.'

'Please Miss Wrench,' Becky began, holding out the silver charm.

'Do I have to repeat myself, Rebecca?' Miss

Wrench cut in. 'The police have enough to do without all you students hanging around!'

The two girls scurried back to their own room.

'What shall we do?' demanded Becky. 'We can't hand the charm in till tomorrow, can we?'

'No. Perhaps we should hold on to it for a little while longer anyway,' Cassie said, thoughtfully.

'All right,' said Becky. 'I'd better lock it up in my little jewellery case.'

When the silver ballerina was safely under lock and key, they quickly grabbed their ballet shoes and dashed off down the stairs.

As she hurried along, Cassie realised she had forgotten all about feeling homesick. There was nothing like a mystery to cheer you up.

2

The Figure in White

As Cassie entered the studio, her worries about Grade Five came flooding back. But, almost immediately, Madame Larette took her to one side. Madame was the favourite ballet mistress in the school – she was small, dark-haired and French, and very sympathetic.

'*Ma chérie*,' she murmured. 'You are disappointed with yourself, *non?*'

'Yes, Madame,' agreed Cassie whole-heartedly.

'I will give you another test. Then we will see.'

'Oh, thank you, Madame! I'll try harder next time.'

'*Non, non*. Not so 'ard next time. Just nice and

easy. Next Thursday, at 'alf past twelve.'

Cassie flew to the barre as though she had grown wings. A second chance! Madame was being very kind to her. Cassie took part in the lesson with a feeling of great relief and happiness and it was Becky, not she, who noticed the black look on Amanda's face.

When they were doing Maths later that morning, Miss Eiseldown gave them a new project to tackle. Their group included Cassie, Becky, Emily and Matthew, a bright, energetic, dark-eyed boy who had come to Redwood without training but who was now a very talented dancer. They were to design a new board game for four players, to play with dice.

Cassie quickly came up with the idea of a ghost train, which the others thought was really good. As the four children started sketching designs, Amanda came past their table and had a crafty peep.

Matthew nudged Cassie once she'd moved away.

'Bet you anything they come up with something similar,' he whispered.

Emily leaned across the table. 'Did you see anything interesting this morning?' she asked.

'Yes,' whispered Cassie. 'But it's hush-hush.'

'Oh,' groaned Matthew. 'That's guaranteed to make us incredibly curious.'

'Well, keep it to yourself,' warned Becky.

'I shall. Promise.'

'And me,' said Emily.

14

'Well, we know *you* will, Em,' Cassie said. 'But there are *others* among us who might not be so trustworthy.'

'Oh come on, Cassie,' Matthew pleaded.

'All right then,' said Cassie, 'but you mustn't tell a soul.' She drew Emily and Matthew closer to her, so she could lower her voice even further. 'We found a silver charm – a little ballerina – right under the cabinet!'

Emily looked anxious when she heard the full story.

'I think you should hand it in,' she said.

'No, Miss Wrench didn't want to know, so let's hang on to it for a while,' said Cassie. 'It might be a clue. We could do some detective work of our own – and I know just where to start!'

Matthew's ears pricked up. 'This sounds interesting.'

'We've got enough detectives already, thanks,' Cassie said quickly.

'Oh, great,' said Matthew. 'I know when I'm not wanted.'

When lunch-time came, Cassie suggested a walk across the grounds.

'I think you were a bit hard on Matthew,' said Emily.

Cassie shrugged. 'He'll get over it.'

'Where are we heading?' asked Becky. The three girls had already crossed the lawns and were level with the folly. From here they could see the cottage which belonged to their friend, Mrs Allingham, nestling in the woods. She had been the one who had come to Emily's rescue last term, when Emily could not afford to replace worn ballet shoes and uniform. The Allingham Bursary had been awarded to Emily to cover the cost of all her equipment.

The girls often did odd jobs for the old lady.

'This is the first bit of our inquiry,' said Cassie.

'How do you mean?'

Cassie paused to gaze at the ruined folly, which had so captured her imagination when she first started ballet school.

'Oh,' she said, 'finding out all we can about Petrakova from Mrs Allingham.'

'Do you think that'll help?'

'You just never know. It might give us a lead; it might not.'

They walked through the tall rhododendron bushes and through the edge of a copse. When they reached the small, ivy-covered cottage, Mrs Allingham's head was visible over her beech hedge. She beamed when she saw them approaching.

'Hello girls. I *have* missed you over the holidays!'

April showers and sunshine had done their work on the cottage garden. Becky gently took the garden fork from her. 'You shouldn't be bending over,' she tutted. Mrs Allingham suffered from arthritis: her ankles and knuckles were quite swollen with it. Cassie sometimes found it hard to imagine that their elderly friend used to be a dancer, and then a ballet teacher at Redwood.

'We've come to do some gardening for you,' said

16

Cassie. 'Looks as though your lawn needs mowing.'

The three girls did as much tidying up as they could in the remainder of their lunch-break and finished with a quick glass of lemonade and an oaty biscuit.

When Cassie told the old lady about the theft of Petrakova's ballet shoe, Mrs Allingham was very shocked.

'Did you know Petrakova at all?' asked Cassie.

'Know her!' she exclaimed. 'Of course I knew Anna. I taught her back in the Sixties. She was our best pupil.'

'Did she become *very* famous?' asked Emily.

Mrs Allingham nodded. 'She was a truly great ballerina, dear. I feel privileged to have been her teacher.'

'If she was younger than you, how come she's dead?' asked Cassie, rather bluntly.

'And I'm not, do you mean?' laughed Mrs Allingham.

'No, no,' said Cassie, blushing. 'I didn't mean it like that!'

'Poor Anna died tragically young. She was only thirty-three. And at the height of her fame. It will be twelve years ago this summer.'

'How sad!' said Becky. 'How did she die?'

'Blood poisoning, they said. She was staying in Mexico at the time.'

'Mexico?' repeated Cassie. 'Was she dancing there?'

'No, I don't think so. She was taking a long

holiday there with her husband, as I remember.'

'Who was he – her husband?'

'I know nothing about him, except that he was in the art world. I don't even know his name, because Anna always kept her stage-name.'

'Oh, wasn't Petrakova her real name, then?' asked Becky.

'No, it was Peters. Anna Peters. Quite English. But she wanted a Russian-sounding name, as she admired the great Russian dancers so, and it *did* sound more glamorous than Peters, don't you think?'

The girls set off back to school, making up suitable stage-names for themselves on the way.

'I'll be Rebecca Hastingavitch,' said Becky.

'And I'll be Cassandra Bruninskia,' giggled Cassie.

Emily frowned. 'I'd want to change Emily to Emmalina, but whatever could you do with Pickering?'

'What about Pickerova?' said Cassie.

The other two collapsed in hysterics at the suggestion. 'It sounds like you're hunting for fleas!' cried Becky.

It wasn't until tea-time that Cassie managed to get Emily and Becky on their own again.

'This fisherman's pie is gorgeous,' said Becky. 'And did you notice there's cheesecake among the puddings? I'll have to get through this fast or there'll be none left.'

'Hang on a minute,' said Cassie. 'I want to tell

you what I think we should do tonight.'

'Tonight?' echoed Emily.

'Tonight.'

'It won't get us into trouble, will it?'

'No, of course not, if we're careful. Are you with me, Becky?'

'Yes, why not? Hurry up, Cassie, I want to go for my pudding.'

'Well, I think we should go down to the entrance hall after all the staff have gone to bed and take it in turns to keep watch.'

'What for?' asked Emily.

'Well, if it *is* just a prank, whoever it is will have been frightened to death by the Wrench this morning and want to return the bronze as soon as possible.'

'But what if it's a serious theft?'

'Haven't you ever heard that the criminal often returns to the scene of the crime?'

'Yes, but why?' Becky asked.

'If the silver ballerina belongs to the thief, she might just come looking for it, mightn't she?'

'Why do you think it's a she?' asked Emily.

'Not many boys have silver charm bracelets, do they?' said Cassie.

'How long do we have to stay in the hall?' asked Becky.

'Well, all night, if we can manage it.'

'All night!' exclaimed Becky. 'I need my beauty sleep!'

'Two of us can catnap while one keeps watch.'

'That's not my idea of a good night's sleep!'

'Nor mine,' agreed Emily, ruefully.

It took all Cassie's powers of persuasion, and the rest of the evening, to get round Emily's and Becky's objections. They only agreed in the end when Cassie bribed them with the promise of a bag of fudge each.

Cassie thought it safe to sleep for the first few hours after lights-out at eight-thirty, although Becky was the only one of the three who managed it. Cassie switched off her watch alarm just before it was due to go off at eleven o'clock. She felt wide awake – it had been torture lying there waiting for the hours to tick by. Becky was quite difficult to rouse, and Cassie was frightened that at any moment they would wake Amanda – at one point she did seem to stir, but then lay quiet again.

At last Becky was sufficiently awake to put on her dressing-gown and slippers and follow Cassie, her pillow under her arm, to collect Emily. After a quiet tap on her door, Emily joined them on the landing.

'What's the pillow for?' she whispered.

'To make sleeping easier,' hissed Becky.

The three girls crept down the stairs and across the deserted school, only using Emily's torch when it was absolutely necessary. In the entrance hall, the chandelier glimmered eerily as moonlight fell upon it. They hid themselves behind a large oak settle near the stone fireplace and almost at once

Becky curled up on the floor and laid her head down on the pillow.

'It's got to be you or me for first watch then,' said Cassie.

'I'll go first,' said Emily. 'I don't feel tired yet. I'll wake you in a couple of hours.'

Cassie knew she wouldn't sleep, so she decided to sit up with Emily. They were both glad of their dressing-gowns. The night was quite chilly and sitting still made them feel even colder.

'Oh, for a hot water bottle,' murmured Emily.

'Becky's fast asleep already,' said Cassie.

The minutes felt more like hours. Everything was still and quiet. They started to get cramping pains in their legs from staying in one position, but they were reluctant to move about, just in case they frightened off the thief. But in the end, they had to get up. They both had terrible pins and needles and felt exhausted and bitterly cold.

Moonlight shone on the wall, touching the rows of photos and finally illuminating the unearthly white of Giselle's costume in the Petrakova portrait. Cassie stared up at the tragic face and pose of the great dancer, which portrayed the unhappy spirit of Giselle, and then remembered with a shudder that the dancer herself had died tragically too.

As they stamped about as quietly as they could, to get their blood circulating again, Cassie heard a noise above, on the staircase. She quickly drew Emily back into a shadowy corner and put a finger to her friend's lips, to warn her not to speak.

They both looked across to the sweeping staircase, which was faintly lit from an overlooking window. Cassie's heart started to race as a figure came into view. Was this their thief? Or something altogether worse?

The figure came slowly down the stairs, so slowly that it seemed unreal. Cassie blinked. The figure was still there. Emily squeezed Cassie's hand in excitement. At the bottom, the figure turned towards them. For an anxious moment, Cassie thought they had been seen, but then realised that the girl (she could now see that it was a first year called Grace) wasn't really seeing anything.

She was sleep-walking.

'How disappointing!' Cassie hissed.

'Shall we take her back upstairs?' suggested Emily.

'Yes. I've had enough. What about you?'

'Yes, me too. I'll go and wake Becky.'

Cassie guided Grace, as Emily followed with the almost equally unconscious Becky back up the grand staircase.

About halfway up, something at the top caught the corner of Cassie's eye. Something white. Another figure, only this one wasn't sleep-walking. It was moving very fast, almost gliding, out of sight. Cassie shivered and turned to her two friends.

'Did you see that?'

'What?'

'That white thing that just flitted across the top of the staircase!'

But neither had seen anything. Cassie wondered

if her mind was playing tricks on her, as she was so tired. All in all, she felt very disappointed at the way the watch had turned out.

Emily offered to take Grace back to her room, and Cassie gratefully ushered Becky back into their bedroom. Luckily Amanda seemed to be sleeping like a log. In the darkness, Cassie could just make out the humped shape of her quilt.

Bed had never seemed so delicious. The sleepwalker and the figure in white were both quickly forgotten as Cassie sank into a deep, dreamless sleep.

3

Old Friends

The mystery was forgotten the next day, when Emily put her head round the door and grinned. 'Have you heard the news? Madame has a migraine and Miss Wrench is taking our ballet class.'

'Oh no!' the friends groaned together.

But Emily was right. When they entered the studio, even the pianist looked tense. All the girls stood silently at the barre. Strains of music came from the studio next door, where the boys' class was already under way.

Miss Wrench stood beside the piano, clutching the stick which she always used when teaching. Today she wore a loose, grey, silk blouse and a very full accordion-pleated skirt.

She rapped her stick on the wooden floor three times. Everyone stood even straighter than before. The pianist, looking terrified, began rearranging his music with fluttering hands.

'Pliés. Ten demi-pliés, ten full pliés in each position, demi-tournant, repeat on the other side.' And to the pianist: 'waltz, page eight.'

The poor man immediately dropped the music and Miss Wrench tapped her foot impatiently while he picked it up.

Halfway through their exercises at the barre, Miss Wrench started to walk up and down, tapping a wayward back foot here and there with her stick. She suddenly stopped beside Becky.

'Tie your ribbons more tidily, girl,' she snapped. 'You should try to copy Amanda. Amanda never has so much as a hair out of place.'

As Becky bent down to tuck in the loose ends which had become dislodged, Miss Wrench moved across to Emily.

'I'm glad to see you're still maintaining a high standard in your appearance. Well done.'

Cassie came to with a start, when she realised Miss Wrench was standing next to her. She had an unfortunate reputation for daydreaming and Miss Wrench had caught her at it once again.

'Cassandra, how many times must we tell you; a dancer must concentrate *at all times*!'

'Sorry, Miss Wrench.'

Cassie felt great relief when the Principal moved

away, but unfortunately she hadn't finished with Becky. During the next exercise, in the centre, she stopped the class and turned on Becky.

'Do you call those développés?'

'No, Miss Wrench,' murmured Becky, looking at her feet.

'Amanda, can you demonstrate the exercise, for the benefit of Rebecca?'

'Yes, certainly, Miss Wrench,' said Amanda, quickly moving forward. The pianist began again and Amanda showed off her développés devant, ending each one in a beautiful fourth croisé plié.

'Thank you, Amanda. That is what I call a développé. Now, everyone, again, please!'

At the end of class, Becky was feeling decidedly grumpy.

'The Wrench made me look such a fool,' she complained.

'Never mind,' said Cassie. 'We should have Madame back tomorrow.'

'And Amanda's a stuck-up show-off,' went on Becky, still smarting.

'Mmm, you're right there,' agreed Cassie.

'Oh, I'm longing to get home for the weekend,' said Becky. 'I'm really fed up with dancing, dancing, dancing all day long.'

'Oh cheer up, Becky. We've got the highlight of your day next – Maths!'

'Well, thank goodness for that. Maths and Science lessons keep me sane. But I can't wait to see my pets.'

'I'd never cope with looking after a pet,' Emily remarked. 'I always have so many jobs to do when I'm at home. I don't know how Mum manages without me when I'm here. But at least I'm not a burden to her any more, thanks to Mrs Allingham.'

Amanda was passing by on her way from the changing-room and overheard Emily's last remark.

'Imagine having to rely on *charity*!' she said loudly to Sharon and Sandra, who were walking alongside her. They tittered and stared at Emily as they walked by.

Emily's face grew very pale, but she said nothing, so Cassie bit back the retort she was longing to make. But at supper-time, it was Cassie's turn to suffer Amanda's sense of humour.

She was standing in the queue some way behind Cassie, laughing and whispering with Sharon and Sandra.

As Cassie carried her supper-tray past them, Amanda stuck her foot out and Cassie went flying. So did the tray, the meal and the crockery. When she had picked herself up off the floor, helped by Becky, she was surrounded by a mess of splattered food and broken china. Miss Oakland, who was on supper duty, came marching over.

'Oh, I might have known it would be you, Cassandra Brown,' she said, hands on hips. 'Get it cleared up promptly before anyone else slips over.'

Cassie started to tell her what had happened but bit her lip. It was no use. Miss Oakland would not believe anything bad about Amanda. As she cleared up the mess, Becky went over to Amanda and glared at her.

'If you try that again, I'll go and tell Miss Eiseldown.'

'Tell-tale-tit, your tongue shall split,' Amanda chanted.

'You're acting like a baby!' said Becky.

But Amanda just burst out laughing.

Cassie and Becky were joined by Emily and found a table as far away from Amanda as possible to eat their supper. Between mouthfuls of crunchy salad, Cassie said, 'You know, for once, I'm really glad it's Friday. Home tonight.'

'Me too,' mumbled Becky, who was wading through a plateful of chips. 'No Amanda for three nights!'

'Wouldn't it be great if Emily could be our room-mate, instead of Amanda?' said Cassie.

'No such luck,' grumbled Becky. 'You know the Wrench wouldn't move Amanda unless Amanda asked for it. She thinks the sun shines out of her bottom!'

Cassie and Emily exploded with laughter. Becky never stayed miserable for long.

As Cassie went home that night in her father's car, she told him all about the ballet shoe theft, and what they'd learned from Mrs Allingham about Anna Petrakova.

But Jake Brown had news as well. He was the head of the local primary school, which Cassie used

29

to attend, and it was their Summer Fayre that weekend. There was so much to discuss, that the journey was over in no time, and soon an exhausted Cassie was tucked up in bed.

The next afternoon, Joy Brown listened to Cassie's troubles as she made a batch of wholemeal scones.

'And even though I practised and practised, my legs just wouldn't do what I wanted them to,' Cassie finished with a big sigh.

'I think Madame Larette was right,' said her mum thoughtfully. 'I mean, about trying too hard. You were probably a bag of nerves.'

'But it's never happened to me before. Not even at my audition!'

Cassie's brother, Adam, burst in, muddy and very cheerful, from football practice. Then little Rachel woke from her nap and started to howl. Cassie ran upstairs two at a time to pick her up from her cot. Rachel's howls changed immediately to chuckles. Cassie was her favourite playmate.

Rachel kept Cassie busy most of the afternoon as Joy wanted to carry on with her baking. As she watched her little sister dress up in some of her old dance show costumes, Cassie thought how good it was to be home. There was no pressure here about preparing for exams or about looking scrupulously neat for class. She hadn't even bothered to put a brush through her hair that morning, let alone pull every wisp back into tight plaits. When her hair was hanging loose, it formed little ringlets around her face, which made her look much younger than eleven.

She felt younger too, back with her family. You were on your own somehow, at school. Cassie felt all the responsibilities flowing away from her. She could be a child again here, playing with an even younger child.

She opened up the front of her dolls' house for Rachel to play with. This was a source of endless wonder to the little girl, and only when the tiny dolls had been put to bed for the seventh time did she let Cassie take her downstairs again. By then, the kitchen table had been laid for tea and Jake had come back from shopping.

As they munched through sandwiches and scones, Adam started asking his dad about the School Fayre, and suddenly Cassie had a funny left-out feeling. It had been Cassie's school before Redwood. As if her mum could read her mind, she said, 'You'll be able to see all your old friends.'

After Rachel and Adam had gone to bed, Cassie made a half-hearted attempt at violin practice. She hadn't had much time to practise at school lately and her music teacher was getting exasperated.

'I think I have the answer to your nerves,' said her mum suddenly. 'Yoga.'

'Yoga!' echoed Cassie, putting down her violin. Her mum had no daytime job as Rachel was a full-time occupation in herself, but she did teach yoga classes two evenings a week.

In no time at all, Joy had Cassie on the floor

31

doing a shoulder-stand. As Cassie was already very loose and supple, she managed many of the postures quite easily. But most important, explained her mum, was the deep, even breathing that you had to learn in yoga.

Over the weekend, Cassie practised the sequence which her mother had taught her.

'Wait till Amanda sees this!' she laughed, as she hooked one leg behind her head.

Her mum tutted. 'You really shouldn't compete so much with Amanda,' she warned. 'Just do your best. It doesn't matter what other people are doing round you.'

Sunday turned out sunny and warm. Looking relieved, Jake went over to the school quite early to help set things up, while Joy, assisted by Cassie and Adam, baked frantically for the cake stall.

At the School Fayre that afternoon, Cassie met most of her old gang from the village school, although of course they now went to the senior school in town. They were pleased to see her, and plied her with endless questions about ballet school life. Soon, they broke up into smaller groups. Cassie was left with her old best friend, Katie, and they walked round the school grounds arm-in-arm, stopping to have a go at the coconut shy and the bowling, and then inspecting the stalls for bargains. They hung on till near the end before buying cakes, because they knew they would be reduced. And they were! They bought six fairy cakes each and had just started to eat them when Jake Brown's voice came over the loudspeaker:

'And now for our surprise entertainment! Ladies and gentlemen, boys and girls, I give you the Anna Lakeley School of Dance!'

As applause rippled around the playground, Cassie nearly choked on her glacé cherry.

'It's a surprise, all right! I could *kill* my dad for not telling me!'

'He must be good at keeping secrets,' said Katie. 'I bet you'll feel funny, not dancing with them.'

Indeed she did. She felt quite wrong being a spectator. She even knew the dances they were doing: they were the usual routines that Miss Lakeley reserved for fêtes.

After the first feeling of strangeness had passed, Cassie watched more critically. She had learned a lot in her first year at Redwood, and already she could see she had left her old dancing school far behind. Not only that, but the choreography itself looked corny and stale. At that moment she felt more than ever thankful that she had won her place at Redwood. She saw that however talented she might be, if she had stayed with this small dancing school, she would have had no hope of ever becoming a professional dancer.

At the end of the performance, Cassie dashed over to see her old teacher. Anna Lakeley was as large and motherly as ever and still wore a bright headscarf and looped earrings. She made a big fuss of her ex-pupil, but she was surrounded by a chattering crowd of pupils and their parents, and soon Cassie felt herself being pushed to the edge of the group.

'Goodbye, Miss Lakeley,' she managed to call to her.

'Oh, goodbye, Cassandra. Lovely to see you again. And thank your dad for inviting us.'

Cassie no longer belonged. It was no use pretending. Nor did she belong to the little primary school. But then, neither did her friends. They had all moved on. It was what happened when you were eleven.

She looked round for Katie. She wasn't standing where she'd left her. After a hunt, Cassie found that Katie had returned to her gang. Suddenly Cassie felt shy about approaching them. Their world was not hers.

Jake Brown noticed his daughter on her own and came to her rescue. He put a fatherly arm round her shoulders and steered her to the cake-stall where her mother and Rachel were standing.

'What did you think of the surprise entertainment?' he asked, with a grin.

Cassie's heart was still full of confused feelings, but despite this she managed an answering smile.

The feeling of unfairness grew inside her until she felt she would burst. Why did things have to change, become more complicated? She half-wished herself a toddler again, like Rachel. She so wanted to succeed in dancing, but it was no easy path.

The face of Amanda Renwick came to her then,

with its mocking half-smile. A shock-wave of jealousy flooded through her body, nearly taking her breath away. Was Amanda really the best, better than her?

Cassie wished as hard as she knew how that she should beat Amanda. Then suddenly her dad's voice broke into her thoughts.

'Cassie, here's Katie looking for you.'

She stood up and waved, and Amanda was forgotten for the moment as Cassie ran to join her old friend.

4

A Ghostly Visitor

When the time for the test came the following week, Cassie felt a flutter of nerves in her tummy. She had been practising hard, but not *too* hard, and had not forgotten her session of yoga every morning. She stood quietly now, doing some deep breathing, before knocking and entering the studio.

'*Ma chérie*,' Madame Larette greeted her. 'Now let us see what you can do.'

Half an hour later, Cassie came out of the studio with a smile on her face. She had done well both at the barre and in her centre work, and Madame Larette had told her straight away that she would be entering her for the Grade Five exam.

Grade Five! It had an impressive ring to it. Cassie, Emily, Amanda, Jane and four other girls had been placed in the examination class for some intensive coaching. Madame Larette still taught them most of the time, but Miss Wrench took them for two grim hours per week. Cassie was only glad that Becky wasn't present to be picked on. Miss Wrench constantly praised Amanda's work and Cassie began to wonder if she were the only dancer-in-the-making of the whole group.

Certainly, Amanda had a brilliant technique, and had amazing flexibility in her hips and spine. Her leg was always the highest; her back-arch always the lowest. But there was a hardness to her dancing that Cassie disliked. It showed particularly in her arm movements, her port de bras. Cassie couldn't help believing that her own style of dancing was more graceful, but perhaps she was kidding herself.

Weeks of hard work flew by. But despite the pressure, Cassie kept to her routine of yoga exercises every morning. Something, maybe her mum's advice, stopped her doing any yoga while Amanda was in the room.

Amanda was as spiteful and boastful as ever. And she became ten times worse when her group won a little prize in Maths for designing the best board-game: a Ghost Castle. Cassie and Becky were soon sick of hearing about it.

'It's just not fair,' Cassie complained, as she sat

down to eat her lunch with Becky and Emily. 'She stole our idea!'

'I can guess what you're talking about,' Matthew said, coming over to join them. 'What are we going to do about it?'

'There's not a lot we can do!' said Emily. 'They've had the prize and that's that.'

'Let's talk about it later. I want to discuss the mystery of the missing shoe as well!' said Cassie. 'Come to our common room at seven-thirty. Amanda never goes there.'

'See you then,' said Matthew.

At seven-thirty, Matthew peered sheepishly round the door of the Junior girls' common room. Luckily there were only a few first years in there. Second years might have told him to get out. Cassie, Becky and Emily took him into the corner farthest away from the television.

'Listen,' said Cassie. 'What are we going to do about the silver ballerina?'

Matthew was thoughtful. 'You're sure it's silver?'

'Yes, I think so.'

'Well, all silver jewellery has a hallmark. That could tell us where it was made. In fact, I've got a book of hallmarks. If you let me borrow the charm, I could find out for you.'

'That's a good idea!' said Cassie.

'I've got a good idea too,' said Becky. 'About Amanda.'

'What? To get our own back for the competition?' asked Emily.

'Yes, and for being a pain,' said Becky. 'I suggest we find a nice fat, slimy frog and put it in her bed.'

'That's brilliant!' said Cassie, laughing.

'Ugh,' said Emily, squirming at the thought. 'As long as I don't have to touch it!'

'I'll do it,' said Becky happily.

'Well, we can all go and look for one tomorrow lunch-time in the wild area,' said Cassie. 'And *you* can catch it, Becky.'

Becky radiated cheerfulness all the next morning. She was so looking forward to her meeting with the frog and as luck would have it, she was the one to find it. The wild area was an untended part of the grounds, at the opposite end from the folly. It had a small pool and some silver birch trees.

'Oh, the dear little thing,' she said, displaying the frog on her hand to the others. Emily screwed up her nose.

'How can you bear to touch it?' she asked.

'I hope it's not going to be too terrified when Amanda screams at it,' said Becky.

'*If* she screams,' said Matthew.

'She'll scream,' said Cassie, confidently.

Becky carried the frog back to school with great tenderness and care.

'You ought to work with animals,' said Cassie.

'I know,' said Becky. 'I'd love to be a vet.'

'That would really suit you.'

'Yes,' agreed Becky. 'But I'm not sure we do

enough Science here for me to get good grades in my GCSEs.'

'That's years away yet,' said Matthew, laughing.

'We don't want you to leave Redwood,' said Cassie.

Becky smiled. 'No, I'd miss all the fun – night-watches and Amanda being grotty and all that.'

Cassie gave her a friendly shove. 'Come on, you know you'd miss us.'

'Watch it!' warned Becky. 'You'll frighten the frog.'

'As long as the frog frightens Amanda!' said Matthew.

He needn't have worried. When Amanda got into bed that night, her screams were heard all over the girls' wing. Some of the second years from further down the landing, with Miss Eiseldown hot on their heels, came rushing to Cassie's room to see what was happening. There was an explosion of laughter before the housemother got into the room. She was just in time to see Becky catching the terrified frog.

'Whatever's that frog doing in here?' she asked.

'Tha . . . *that* was in my bed,' said Amanda, in a very wobbly voice.

'And who put it there, I wonder?' demanded Miss Eiseldown, staring very hard at Cassie and Becky. Cassie couldn't meet her eyes and found to her consternation that she was blushing.

'Go and put the poor thing outside at once, Rebecca!'

'Yes, Miss Eiseldown.'

'And you'd both better have black marks. I *won't* have these disturbances on my landing. If you cause another one this term, I shall send you straight to Miss Wrench. Is that understood?'

'Yes, Miss Eiseldown,' said Cassie and Becky in a bleaty kind of chorus.

The housemother shooed the second years back to bed and returned to her own room. Once Becky had gone out with the frog, Cassie was left alone to face a very cross Amanda.

'I'll get you back for this, Cassandra Brown,' she spat out. 'You think you're so clever, don't you?'

'Not really,' said Cassie. 'I think that's more your problem.'

Cassie was relieved when Amanda clamped her mouth tightly shut and got into bed.

In the build-up to the Grade Five exam, Becky was a great friend to have around. She wasn't tense herself, and could talk about lots of non-exam subjects, to take Cassie's mind off it. That, plus yoga, seemed to beat exam nerves, and when the day came, she felt confident, with only a few twinges before breakfast.

'Good luck,' shouted Becky, as she left the dining-hall to go to the studio.

Cassie joined Amanda, Emily and Jane in the girls' changing-room. Cassie had plenty of time to get changed as she was to be called in second. Jane went in first, as her surname was Andrews.

'How did it go?' they all wanted to know when she came out. By now, the girls had joined Matthew and his friends Tom and Ojo, who were also taking the exam, in the small waiting-room. Jane looked ready to burst into tears.

'Not very well!' she said.

Amanda laughed a mocking laugh. 'You just haven't got it in you, Jane. Let's face it.'

Cassie turned on her angrily. 'Oh, shut up, you!' she cried.

Miss Wrench opened the studio door. *'Will you wait quietly*! Next candidate please.'

Cassie walked in, faced her examiner and made a graceful curtsey, hoping that her pounding heart would soon settle down. Her legs trembled as she began her pliés, but she forced herself to breathe more deeply and in time to the music, and soon lost herself in the exercises.

In the centre, she felt she gave a good account of herself in the adage section, but suddenly, when she reached the jumping steps she grew nervous again. She couldn't understand why, until she reached jetés en tournant and remembered that a fortnight ago she had fallen doing this step. A feeling of panic flooded through her.

Telling herself not to be stupid, Cassie took a deep breath and executed the turning, leaping step perfectly. After that she grew in confidence, so that by the time she performed the set classical piece she was completely at ease.

Cassie felt her face relax into a natural smile for

the examiner, who was peering at her intently. She felt her head perfectly poised, her neck long, body pulled up from the hips, as she moved through the opening sequence. At last she was dancing, not just doing exercises. Cassie saw the gleam of approval in the examiner's eye as she held her finishing pose. In the Character dance, which ended the examination, she noticed too how the examiner exchanged meaningful looks with the pianist.

That evening, Cassie managed to finish her homework in homework period. After supper, even though she was tired, she took out her violin. She was feeling guilty about the small amount of time she had spent practising lately. Becky was curled up on her bed with a book about creepy-crawlies and a box of mints. Amanda was sorting through her chest of drawers.

Cassie began to play Brahms' Waltz – hesitatingly at first, but then more fluently.

After a few minutes, Amanda stopped what she was doing. 'Do you *have* to make that awful noise!' she yelled and put her hands over her ears. She stomped out of the room and banged the door shut behind her.

'She doesn't know a good thing when she hears it!' said Becky. 'I'll have to treat her to my cello tomorrow.'

Cassie laughed. 'At least we know now how to get rid of her!'

Becky got out a packet of chocolate wafer biscuits and they settled down to a good guzzle. Amanda still hadn't returned by eight twenty-five.

'I wonder what's happened to her?' asked Cassie.

'She must be staying with Sharon and Sandra,' said Becky. 'But it's not like her to do anything against the rules.'

'Well, she knows we're unlikely to tell Miss Eiseldown,' said Cassie.

As she was changing into her pyjamas, Cassie spotted a folded white handkerchief on the floor, by Amanda's chest of drawers and picked it up. 'Trust Amanda to have her initials on her hankies!' she said. 'She must have dropped this when she was tidying her drawers.'

'Let's have a look!' said Becky. Cassie tossed it over to her. 'Fancy too! But what's the letter after the A? It doesn't look like an R.'

Cassie studied the embroidered initials. 'I think it's a P,' she said. 'Strange!' She placed the hanky on Amanda's chest of drawers and jumped into bed.

'Hope Amanda doesn't come in late and wake us up!' said Becky, with a yawn.

But it wasn't Amanda getting into bed which woke Cassie later. She could just make out Becky's shape in her bed. There was enough moonlight coming through the curtains to see the dark outlines of furniture and the brass handle of the door.

What had woken her? She listened intently. A soft padding on the landing outside. It went past, then returned. It came close, very close. Then stopped.

Cassie's ears were straining. She heard some faint rustling sounds. Then nothing. She waited. Again the rustling sounds.

She sat up in bed and stared at the door, willing herself to see through it. Whatever was making those sounds was right outside. She held her breath.

The brass doorknob rattled and slowly turned. The door eased open slightly. Cassie was wide-eyed. Her heart thumped in her chest.

A hand appeared in the gap. A white, slender hand, with long pale fingers. The index finger was pointing, pointing straight at Cassie.

Before Cassie had a chance to cry out, the disembodied hand had gone, closing the door behind it with a snick. Cassie felt too terrified to do anything but bury her head under her covers and lie there, eyes open in the suffocating darkness, for what seemed like hours.

5

Red Riding Hood

Next morning, Becky had to shake her awake. Cassie was amazed that she had gone back to sleep at all.

'Oh, no,' she groaned. 'It's not time to get up already?'

'Afraid so,' said Becky.

'I've had a terrible night,' Cassie complained. 'There were footsteps on the landing. Then the doorknob turned and the door opened and there was . . .'

'The Wrench?' Becky asked, eyes wide.

'No, that wouldn't have been half as bad!' said Cassie.

'Nothing could be worse, surely?' laughed Becky.

'Shut up, Becky and listen! It was horrible. A hand, with the finger pointing at me!' Cassie shuddered.

'Just a bad dream,' said Becky cheerfully. 'You were probably a bit worked up after your exam.'

Luckily the day that followed was so busy that Cassie was able to put the ghostly visit to the back of her mind. At breakfast, Emily was the herald of news that filled Cassie with great excitement. The annual Gala performance, put on by the Upper School, was to be *The Sleeping Beauty* this year, and there were to be two parts offered to the Juniors – one for a boy and one for a girl.

'The auditions are tomorrow,' said Emily. 'And anyone who wants to try for a part will be taught the dance today in class.'

As it turned out, everyone who had just taken Grade Five wanted to audition, so Madame Larette taught the whole group – boys and girls together – the parts of Red Riding Hood and the Wolf. This Character dance was in Act Three of the ballet.

They were not difficult parts to learn, but what made them interesting was the element of melodrama. The boys especially had great fun acting and dancing the wolf. Matthew had never looked happier in ballet class. Red Riding Hood's was a pretty little dance, with quite nifty footwork in places, and Cassie fell in love with it.

'If only we all had a chance to dance it,' she thought. There would be stiff competition because several students from the second year were also going to audition, she'd heard. And Amanda, of course.

After class, Cassie and Emily were discussing the part in the changing room when Amanda walked in. 'I really shouldn't bother going in for Red Riding Hood if I were you,' she sneered. 'You don't stand a chance.'

'Don't be so sure of yourself,' countered Cassie. 'You don't know how good the second years are.'

'Hah,' scoffed Amanda. 'They'll be looking for someone small and sweet – most of the second years look gawky.'

Just then, Sharon called to her, and the two girls went off together.

Cassie and Emily were both left feeling deflated. They knew only too well that Amanda was Miss Wrench's favourite pupil.

'It's just a waste of time, isn't it?' said Emily.

'No, no,' said Cassie. 'We mustn't think like that. Madame Larette would be furious if she heard you.'

'Oh well,' said Emily. 'At least it's a really nice dance to learn.'

The Juniors were also going to present their own ballet at the Gala at the end of term, but theirs would be danced at the matinée, not the evening performance. The first years were going to present an underwater ballet, set to part of *The Planets* by Holst. Madame Larette had choreographed it herself, and the children were going to design and make their own set and props in Art class, and their own costumes in Needlework.

Madame Larette gave out parts in the afternoon class. She had designed the piece so that everyone had their fair share of dancing. The majority of the girls were sea-nymphs, each with a lovely name, whereas the boys were going to play more humorous or energetic characters, such as an octopus or two swordfish. Cassie was to be a nymph called Nerine and Emily a nymph called Ursula. Becky didn't like the idea of being a sea-nymph at all and so, after a hurried conversation with Madame, was allowed to be a lobster.

At the end of class, Madame Larette quickly rehearsed the few who were going to audition for Little Red Riding Hood.

'Remember – sweetness and innocence!' she told the girls as they made their curtseys at the end of the rehearsal.

Art lessons had never been so exciting before. Becky and Cassie were given the task of making a lobster pot.

Matthew came over to admire their handiwork. They, in turn, had to go and admire his – a portion of the backdrop which he was painting in beautiful rich shades of blue and green.

In Needlework, all the nymphs had a basic Greek tunic shape to work from, but they could choose their own material and decoration. Cassie chose coral pink, which she thought would contrast well with the backdrop. Becky's and Matthew's costumes looked much more difficult to make and their teacher spent most of her time with them. Cassie couldn't really understand why Becky wanted to be a lobster.

'I suppose she thinks it's more fun,' suggested Emily, who was busy cutting out pieces of turquoise material. When they looked across to Becky's table, she and Matthew were indeed in fits of giggles about Matthew's octopus costume.

Hoots of laughter came again from Becky's table as Matthew threw his green material over his head, and groped around making spooky noises.

'Oh, don't!' Cassie shivered. 'That's reminded me of my nightmare.' She told Emily all about it.

'A pointing finger!' cried Emily. 'Why ever did you dream about that?'

'I don't know,' said Cassie. 'I'm not even sure it was a dream. I just hope it doesn't ever come back.'

'No,' agreed Emily, 'you'll need a good night's sleep tonight. Auditions tomorrow!'

Cassie slept like a log that night. Becky again had to wake her up at seven. The day promised to be very warm. Streams of sunlight fell into the room from their window.

Taking a few minutes to come round, Cassie lay thinking about the audition which lay before her that morning. Would she remember the steps? Would she be able to present the character of Red Riding Hood well enough? She felt more nervous than before her exam, which she knew was silly.

Much calmer after doing a sequence of yoga postures, she went along with Becky to breakfast, calling for Emily on the way.

'Are you nervous?' asked Emily. 'I am.'

'Not too bad,' said Cassie. 'Though I wish it wasn't the Wrench taking the audition.'

'I don't know why we're bothering really,' said Emily. 'Everyone knows she'll pick Amanda.'

'Even the Wrench has to be fair over auditions, surely?' said Cassie.

'Why should she be?' countered Becky. 'She's her own boss after all. Who's going to argue with her?'

Cassie sighed. There was a lot of truth in what Becky was saying. But she knew that whatever the outcome, it was really important to do her best. Everything counted. There were so many dancers wanting to make it that you could never afford to relax or be slipshod in your attitude.

Their first academic lesson of the day was Maths. They were doing co-ordinates and Cassie kept getting her x and y axes mixed up, even though Becky tried to explain where she was going wrong. Miss Eiseldown had to go through the topic with her step by step. Then she turned to Becky.

'You've finished your work in record time,' she said.

'I love Maths and Science!' said Becky.

Miss Eiseldown laughed. 'Well, you're the exception in this school.'

'In more ways than one,' muttered Becky.

'Aren't you happy here, Becky?'

'Mostly, but I want to be a vet. What's dancing got to do with that?'

'Well, nothing directly. But ballet gives you poise and an understanding of music and rhythm which will make you a more well-rounded person,' said Miss Eiseldown. 'Really, it doesn't matter at all that you don't want to take up dancing as a career.'

'Try telling my mum that!' said Becky.

'Only a very small proportion of our students ever get to be professional dancers,' said Miss Eiseldown. 'You're in a more fortunate position than most, Becky. I'll make sure you get all the help you need to fulfil your ambition.'

'Thank you, Miss Eiseldown,' was all Becky could manage to say. But her shining eyes expressed her gratitude more eloquently.

Next lesson was History, but the candidates for audition had to excuse themselves, which didn't go down very well with their History teacher. In the dance studio, they were asked to sit against the end wall, and were called in pairs. Of course, there were fewer boys, so they had to do the dance more than once, with different partners. Matthew had to dance the Wolf four times in all, but he enjoyed every minute of it.

Cassie was pleased to find that he was her partner when she was called. But as she tiptoed forwards, miming the journey Red Riding Hood takes through the wood, picking flowers on her way, Cassie was conscious only of Miss Wrench's eyes upon her. To please her was everything at this moment. The thought unsettled her and she felt she went through the dance like a puppet.

Miss Wrench made no comment after anyone's presentation, but Madame Larette thanked each dancer and found words of praise for everyone. Matthew's ballet master, Mr Turner, standing next to Madame, helped the students to forget their nerves by cracking funny jokes.

'Why did the fly fly?' he demanded of Emily. Emily giggled and shook her head.

'Because the spider spied her!' he shouted.

Miss Wrench looked disapproving, but Mr Turner seemed not to notice.

The pianist took comfort from Mr Turner's humour, and played far more confidently than usual. The dramatic music inspired most of the young dancers to do their very best. There were some wonderful girl dancers in the second year – Cassie wouldn't like to have to choose between them. But the three second year boys were all fairly weak. There was no doubt in her mind that Matthew's performance out shone all the rest.

After the last second year had danced, they were sent back to lessons, on tenterhooks. The staff were going to discuss the audition and let them know the result later. Amanda was unbearable for the rest of the day. She looked so smug, as though she already knew she had got the part. Cassie sat in lessons with her fingers and ankles crossed most of the day. How she would love to dance in *The Sleeping Beauty* with the sixth-formers!

* * *

54

It was Emily, as always, who brought the news.

'It's been posted up!' she cried.

'Don't tell me,' gulped Cassie. 'I want to look for myself.'

She went down the stairs two at a time and raced along the corridor to the notice-board. There in black and white were the results of the audition:

Red Riding Hood . . .Amanda Renwick, year 1
The Wolf . . .Matthew Smith, year 1

Cassie shrugged and looked at Emily. 'You were right,' she said. 'We needn't have bothered.'

'But you did very well,' said Emily. 'Congratulations!'

'What for?' asked Cassie in surprise.

'Haven't you read it all?' laughed Emily. In smaller print, at the bottom of the notice, it said:

Understudies . . .Cassandra Brown, year 1
Paul Richmond, year 2

But somehow, it made no difference at all to Cassie's intense feeling of disappointment.

'How do *you* feel, Emily?' she asked her friend.

'I really wasn't expecting to get the part,' said Emily, 'but I thought you were better than Amanda.'

'Miss Wrench obviously didn't think so,' replied Cassie, 'but thanks anyway. Come to think of it – I thought you made a better job of it than Amanda, too.'

Emily laughed. 'Come on, Cassie. Cheer up. At least you'll get to go to the rehearsals.'

Thinking about it, Cassie realised that this was indeed a bonus – she would get to know *The Sleeping Beauty* inside out. She already loved Tchaikovsky's music for the ballet, and it would be great fun to watch the Upper School students dancing. The Juniors didn't often have the chance.

Feeling decidedly better, she faced the day ahead of her without too many twinges of envy when she looked in Amanda's direction.

The lesson she most enjoyed that day was Character class. The girls all slipped on their calf-length black skirts and special black shoes and entered the studio, where they curtsied to Mrs Bonsing, their teacher for this class. Mrs Bonsing was a very jolly, round, middle-aged woman, who was amazingly light on her feet. Although she was plump, her hands and feet were as tiny as a child's and her agility astonishing.

She was teaching them the Hornpipe and this energetic, rhythmical dance was just the antidote Cassie needed for her disappointment. As she bounced up and down, heel and toe, heel and toe, 'climbed the rigging' and 'hauled in the ropes', Cassie's eyes began to shine and her cheeks to glow. When she had the chance to look around, she saw that all the other girls looked happy and invigorated. Ballet was so lovely, but the constant repetitive exercises could be quite tedious at times. Character class was a welcome break.

In fact, Cassie loved all her classes, including Contemporary and Jazz, unlike Emily, who only really liked Classical Ballet, and Becky, who much preferred Character dancing to anything else.

The next two weeks were crammed with rehearsals for the Juniors' underwater ballet, but the sixth years were only practising the first act of *The Sleeping Beauty*, so Amanda, Cassie and Matthew hadn't been needed as yet.

Then one morning, the results of the Grade Five examination were posted up. Emily and Jane came hurtling into Cassie's room before breakfast to tell her.

'Cassie!' Emily blurted out breathlessly. 'Guess what! You've got—'

'Stop!' yelled Cassie imperiously, clamping her hand firmly over her friend's mouth. 'I've told you before, I like to see for myself!'

Amanda sniggered behind her. 'I don't know why you're being so fussy. Of course, if you'd done as well as I have, you'd want everyone to know!'

The other girls looked at her curiously.

'Have you seen the board already then?' asked Emily.

'No, I just heard,' said Amanda mysteriously.

'Come on then, tell us how you did,' said Becky wearily.

'Top marks,' said Amanda with a self-satisfied smile. 'Ninety-two per cent.'

Cassie already had one foot out of the door. Amanda's result made her catch her breath, but she resolutely turned her back and raced down to the notice-board. She was delighted to find she had also gained a Distinction, with eighty-nine per cent, the same mark as Matthew. Emily and the other girls had passed with Merit.

Madame Larette was terribly pleased with all of them, giving each a big hug.

'Congratulations, *mes chéries*,' she said, beaming. 'You deserve all the success.'

Becky was thrilled for her friends, too. In fact there were only two things which blemished Cassie's happiness: one was a pang that Amanda had outdone her yet again; the other was that the mystery of Petrakova's bronze ballet shoe had still not been solved.

6

Midnight Meeting

Matthew had been sky-high with excitement all week about getting the part of the Wolf, and, after he had had his exam result, he was determined to celebrate. When the girls bumped into him and his friend Tom after ballet class on Saturday morning, he couldn't wait to tell them his idea.

'Let's have a midnight feast tonight, to celebrate. I've got loads of pocket money stashed away.'

'Great idea!' said Becky immediately. 'We can buy what we need when we go into the village after lunch.'

Cassie and Emily were equally enthusiastic.

'But where are we going to meet?' asked Cassie.

The boys' block was at the far side of the house and it wouldn't be safe for them to try to visit each other's rooms so late.

'How about the little waiting-room, by the big studio?' asked Tom.

They all thought it sounded a good idea. It would be at quite a distance from the residential members of staff, and was roughly central in the house.

'If we get caught moving about, what shall we say?' asked Emily, a little nervously.

'We won't get caught!' said Matthew confidently.

Miss Oakland approached their group as she was leaving the studio. Becky noticed her from the corner of her eye.

'Shh!' she warned. 'See you at midnight!'

The boys moved off, with a wave.

'Midnight!' breathed Cassie excitedly. There was magic in the word itself.

The reality was more down-to-earth. The alarm went off quietly at twelve under Becky's pillow and neither Cassie nor Becky had the least desire to get out of bed. They dragged themselves out, moving quietly so as not to waken Amanda, wrapped themselves in dressing-gowns, put on slippers, and met Emily outside her door.

It wasn't until they were crossing the central part of the building that the excitement got to them. It came out in fits of suppressed giggles. The boys heard them coming and pulled the girls into the room smartly.

'Shh! You three!' said Tom, who was feeling

nervous. 'We don't want to wake the Wrench.'

The three girls managed to stifle their laughter and get down to the serious business of unwrapping the feast. Their shopping expedition had been extravagant. There were iced buns, jam doughnuts, crisps, chocolate biscuits and apple juice. Cassie suddenly felt fully awake and just as hungry as if it were breakfast-time. Becky, who always had an appetite, was already munching a bun. Emily, however, a finicky eater at the best of times, sat and watched the others making pigs of themselves, while she only nibbled at a couple of crisps. Cassie quite quickly felt sick, so it was Becky and the two boys who finished up the bulk of the goodies. Once the eating was over, the friends exchanged a few jokes before Emily began to yawn. This set them all off, one by one.

'Oh, you just can't stand the pace!' said Matthew, stifling his own yawn.

'No, you're right, we can't!' said Becky. 'In fact, if there hadn't been the promise of food, wild horses wouldn't have dragged me out of bed!'

'Ooh, bed!' sighed Emily, 'that sounds nice.'

'Oh, I nearly forgot,' said Matthew, reaching into his pocket. 'You'd better have this back.'

He handed Cassie the silver ballerina. It felt cold on her palm.

'I looked up the hallmark for you. It was stamped in Birmingham.'

'Right,' said Cassie. 'Thanks.' Now they had this piece of information, she wondered what on earth

61

they could do with it. It really didn't get them anywhere!

Feeling quite disappointed, she stood up. 'Come on then. What're we waiting for? The Wrench to find us?'

Becky shivered and got up, pulling Emily up with her. They said goodbye to the boys and made their way back across school towards the girls' wing. On the return journey, they felt too tired to be giggly and too conscious of the dark silence around them to want to speak.

It was funny how everything looked so different in the dark, thought Cassie. All the familiar corridors and rooms, usually so brightly lit, now seemed murky and oppressive in the wan rays of moonlight which the high windows let in. Cassie was glad that their journey wouldn't take them through the entrance hall, with its dark oak panelling and furniture and grand staircase. She remembered with a shudder how spooky it had seemed during their night-watch.

It was a relief to reach their own staircase. As they rounded the head of it, she stumbled into Becky, who had stopped abruptly in front of her.

'What?' hissed Cassie.

'Shh!' warned Becky, pointing straight ahead. Cassie, now joined by Emily, looked along the landing. Just vanishing around the end of it was a figure dressed all in white.

The girls huddled together for a moment, too frightened to do anything else. Then Cassie found her voice.

'It's what I saw that night at the top of the main staircase.'

'Was it a g-ghost?' whispered Emily.

'I don't fancy following it to find out, anyway,' said Cassie. She was shaking.

'Bet you it's someone playing tricks,' said Becky.

'I don't want to go back to my room,' said Emily. 'The others'll be asleep.'

'Come with us,' said Cassie. 'You can share my bed.'

They crept back into their room and into bed. Amanda lay rock still, under a mounded quilt.

'I wonder if Redwood *is* haunted?' whispered Cassie. 'Perhaps that wasn't a dream I had the other night, after all.'

Cassie was so glad of the comfort of Emily beside her, that she managed to drift into sleep surprisingly quickly. The last thing she remembered hearing was a quiet *snick*, before sinking into dreams about *The Sleeping Beauty*.

When she opened her eyes the next morning, Amanda was standing over her, hands on hips.

'What's Emily doing in here?' she demanded.

Cassie stretched and yawned. 'Oh, she had a nightmare and was too frightened to stay in her room.'

'Come off it,' said Amanda. 'I heard you all prowling about in the middle of the night. What were you up to, eh?'

'I didn't think we'd disturbed you,' replied Cassie warily. 'We weren't *up* to anything in particular.'

63

Amanda sniffed and went off to the bathroom.

The three friends washed, dressed and sauntered down to the dining-hall for breakfast, where they were joined by Matthew and Tom. They all felt tired, but Sunday was a fairly quiet day, so it didn't matter.

Becky seemed to have caught a cold, and looked red-eyed. The boys were bleary-eyed too and rather quiet, but they woke up quite quickly when Cassie started to tell them about the ghost.

'And it just vanished round the corner of the landing,' interrupted Emily breathlessly.

'Wait a minute,' said Matthew. 'What *is* at the end of the landing?'

'A fire-door,' answered Becky.

'Well, there you are. It was just one of the girls out on a prank like us. She must have decided to go out into the grounds, down the fire-escape.'

The girls laughed. 'Only one thing wrong with that theory,' said Cassie. 'The fire-door is always kept locked now, and the key is in a glass box by the door. You can only get it by breaking the glass.'

'Or stealing one of the teachers' keys,' said Becky, between sneezes.

'So, you think the place is haunted,' said Matthew, in his spookiest voice. Cassie giggled. It was easy to forget now, in the sunlit hall, their fears of the night before.

Cassie spent most of the day catching up with homework, but she finished it in time to do some extra ballet practice.

She felt on top form the next morning, and

excited because rehearsals were starting that afternoon for the wedding act of *The Sleeping Beauty*. Morning lessons seemed three times longer than usual, but at last five o'clock came and Cassie made her way to Studio Two.

She sat in a corner with Matthew and watched the rehearsal get under way. Amanda sat in the opposite corner by herself. Cassie was impressed by the high standard of all the older dancers and sat spellbound as Miss Wrench, assisted by Miss Oakland, made the three members of the first pas de trois repeat small sequences over and over again, until she got the best out of them.

The scene included fairies and fairy-tale characters (such as Red Riding Hood and the Wolf), who were the guests at Aurora's wedding. After the first fairy dances came some of the character pieces. First was the dance of the White Cat and Puss in Boots, then the two Bluebirds had their turn. Cassie loved the music for this pas de deux and tried to memorise each bird-like movement of the arms, and every graceful leap. She especially enjoyed the boy Bluebird's solo – he was a talented dancer and his elevation was remarkable. During his jetés and sissonnes, he seemed to hang in mid-air for a moment. It was obvious why he had been chosen for the part.

Cassie was startled when the music began for Red Riding Hood to run through the wood. She suffered a pang or two as Amanda danced across the studio, but tried to ignore her and watch

Matthew instead. He tackled the part of the Wolf with his usual energy and enthusiasm, but when the two of them danced together Cassie couldn't blot out Amanda, and felt downright jealous.

Then, at last came bliss – the pas de deux which Cassie had been waiting for, between the Prince and Aurora. The pair who were dancing the principal parts were called David and Lydia, and Cassie felt sure that they must have a future on the stage. Their dance ended in a series of spectacular turns and 'fish-dives', accompanied by music of mounting excitement. The Prince's solo was full of energetic leaps, and, like the Bluebird dancer, David managed to give the effect of being suspended for a few moments before landing softly. Aurora returned for her solo, which was dainty and precise, showing off the femininity of the dancer. How Cassie admired her! Lydia had such poise and presence. You felt you *had* to watch her once she started to dance. Would she ever get that far herself, she wondered? The majority of Lower School students never made it into the Upper School at all.

Cassie was amazed when Miss Wrench said that was all they had time for that day.

Never mind, she told herself. *It's been lovely to watch all these older dancers.*

'Hi!' said Matthew, appearing in front of her. 'Did you enjoy that?'

'Yes!' she cried enthusiastically. 'And you were great, Mat!'

'It feels like tea-time. Come on, Casablanca, last one to the dining-hall's a mouldy cabbage!'

As they moved towards the door, Miss Oakland intercepted them.

'Matthew, Miss Wrench wants me to correct a couple of errors in your dance. Can you meet me in Room 21 at seven-thirty for a bit of coaching?'

'Yes, fine, Miss Oakland.'

'Don't forget!'

The teacher walked off to another group of students. Matthew turned to Cassie, who was staring after Miss Oakland.

'Well, that's a let-down. I thought I was perfect already!' He laughed, but Cassie didn't respond. 'What's the matter?'

'Did you see what she had on her wrist?' she asked, in a strangled voice.

'No,' said Matthew.

'A silver charm bracelet!'

'Right,' said Matthew. 'This *is* interesting!'

Cassie couldn't wait to tell Becky and Emily and ran all the way to the dining-hall, despite the danger of being spotted by a teacher and given a black mark or worse.

'Guess what?' she burst out when she'd found their table. 'Miss Oakland's chief suspect.'

Becky nearly choked on her chips. 'Miss *Oakland*?' she repeated. Cassie explained about the bracelet.

'I can't imagine Miss Oakland being a thief,' laughed Emily.

'You can laugh,' said Cassie, rather huffily. 'But

it's the best lead we've had for ages.'

'Yes, it'll lead us up the garden path!' giggled Becky.

Cassie swallowed an angry retort. She hated being laughed at. She left her friends and joined the end of the supper queue. As luck would have it, she was standing right behind Amanda.

'Ah, the understudy,' said Amanda.

Cassie bristled. 'Better that than a second-rate Red Riding Hood,' she countered. Amanda's nostrils flared and she tossed her head angrily.

'I don't think Miss Wrench would agree with you.'

'Oh shut up, Amanda,' said Cassie. Before Amanda could say anything else, Cassie spotted Matthew waving at her from further along the line, and nipped over to him.

'You look flushed,' Matthew remarked. Cassie coloured up even more. 'I'm just sick of Amanda,' she explained. 'She takes every opportunity she can to put me down.'

'Don't worry about it,' said Matthew. 'What did the others think about you-know-who?'

'Oh, not very impressed. I need a closer look at that bracelet, to see if anything's missing.'

Privately, Cassie resolved to investigate Miss Oakland as thoroughly as possible. She had a lead, that was the main thing, and she wasn't going to let it go.

7

Chief Suspect

As luck would have it, Miss Oakland took their ballet class the next morning. Disappointingly, she wasn't wearing any jewellery. Cassie had half-expected this, as the ballet teachers rarely did when they were taking class.

It was an uneventful class. Miss Oakland was sarcastic to several girls, but not as bitingly as sometimes, and not to Cassie or her friends. Cassie kept thinking about her investigation, but her mind was crystal sharp, enabling her to concentrate well on her dancing also.

Cassie brought up the subject of the bracelet again at break-time.

'She's the only one we've seen with a charm bracelet!' said Cassie.

'You shouldn't jump to conclusions,' warned Becky.

'Anyway,' sighed Cassie, feeling rather frustrated with Becky's caution, 'are we agreed she's chief suspect for the moment?'

The girls nodded.

'And further investigation is needed?'

'Yes, but—' began Becky.

'We must keep a very close watch on Miss Oakland and try to get a closer look at her bracelet to see if a charm's missing.'

'I don't know,' said Emily. 'We could get into heaps of trouble if she thought we were following her.'

'Oh, don't be such a wimp,' said Cassie. 'She won't notice. And just think, we may solve the mystery!'

Emily sighed. 'I suppose so.'

Madame Larette was waiting in the studio when the girls walked in. They made a curtsey to her and took their places at the barre. After their warming-up exercises, which could never be hurried, Madame announced the start of the rehearsal for the Gala. Today she would concentrate on the group dance of the sea-nymphs, which involved nearly all the girls present. She placed them in the starting positions she wanted, in clusters of three and four, and then taught them an enchaînment of steps, slowly first, then up to tempo, bringing in the piano accompaniment. Even while she was concentrating hard on the new sequence, Cassie thought to herself how lovely it must be to choreograph dances like this, like painting pictures with dancers instead of paint. She was looking forward to tuition in choreography which they would all receive in the third year.

Madame's voice broke into her thoughts. 'Now, that is the opening number. There will be a couple of solos next, for the nymphs Nerine and Ursula.'

With a shock of pleasure, Cassie remembered that she and Emily were dancing those parts. She looked across at her friend, and they exchanged delighted smiles, as Madame Larette went on to say that she would arrange a separate time to teach the girls their solos.

After the lesson, Amanda looked furious. She was speaking in low tones to Sharon and Sandra, but kept looking across at Cassie and Emily.

'Look out,' whispered Emily. 'She's up to no good.'

Cassie had a late extra violin lesson with Mr Green after supper, in preparation for her Grade Three examination. When she got back to her room, Becky wasn't there, but Amanda was waiting for her. The atmosphere was very tense. Cassie thought she'd gather her things together ready for a shower, and get out of Amanda's way, but Amanda was set on confrontation.

'How's the little nymph then?' she sneered.

Cassie pretended not to hear. She was in a good mood, and didn't want to spoil it by rowing with Amanda.

'Goodness knows why they chose you to be *my* understudy. You haven't as much style in your whole body as I've got in my little finger.' Amanda waggled the little finger of her right hand, as though to prove it.

'In fact, I don't know why you're here at all. You'll never be a dancer.' She yawned and stretched out full length on her bed.

'Let's face it – you're just second-rate.'

Cassie held on to her rising temper. 'What's the matter, Amanda? Afraid I'm going to shine in *my* solo?'

Amanda's eyes flashed as she shoved Cassie hard, making her fall back on to the floor. She pinned Cassie down, her breath coming in little gasps of fury.

With a tremendous effort, Cassie pushed her off to one side, but they were very close to the wardrobe and Amanda struck her head as she rolled.

'Ow!' she yelled. 'I'll tell Miss Wrench about this!'

Cassie felt a qualm of anxiety that Amanda would carry out her threat, but pushed it out of her mind.

At that moment, Emily and Becky walked in. Amanda was picking herself up off the floor.

'Oh, here comes the other famous nymph!' said Amanda nastily.

'Oh don't start again!' cried Cassie.

'I'm sure Emily won't fly off the handle like you,'

Amanda continued. 'No, she'll just go off into a corner and feel sorry for herself, won't you, Emily?'

'What's all this about?' asked Emily, looking baffled.

'Never mind,' said Cassie. 'Let's leave Amanda to her bad temper.'

'*My* bad temper!' cried Amanda. '*I* don't go round attacking people.'

'Come on,' said Cassie. 'Let's go.'

As the friends took refuge in Emily's room next door, Cassie told them about Amanda's threat.

'But you could tell the Wrench she started it,' said Emily.

'Oh, Amanda would never get into any trouble. The Wrench always takes her side,' argued Becky.

'That's right,' sighed Cassie. 'I just hope I won't have to share a room with her next term.'

'I shouldn't think you will,' said Emily. 'Everyone gets reshuffled at the beginning of a new year.'

'Even so, she'll still be around, sticking her needles in,' said Cassie wearily.

Becky put an arm round her friend. 'She's really got it in for you, hasn't she? It must be because she sees you as competition. You know, in technique you're the best in the year after her, and you're much more graceful.'

'I don't know about that,' said Cassie.

'Yes, you are, Cassie,' said Emily. 'And Amanda just can't stand you being so good. She's got to be the star. *All* the time.'

'Well, I'm sick of Amanda,' said Cassie. 'Let's do

something. Do you fancy coming up to Miss Oakland's landing now with me?'

Becky shook her head. 'No, I'm having an early night. This cold's getting me down. I feel really tired.'

'OK,' said Cassie. 'How about you, Em? I've just got to get out of this room!'

'Yes, I'll come with you,' said Emily, a little unenthusiastically. You never knew where Cassie's hare-brained schemes would lead.

The two girls watched their ballet teacher's door at a safe distance, hidden in an alcove, for about half an hour. Just when they were about to give up and go to bed, they saw Miss Oakland come out, leaving her door ajar and go down the stairs.

'Aren't we going to follow her?' whispered Emily nervously.

'No, I've got a better idea,' said Cassie, suddenly feeling reckless. 'Let's look in her room!'

'Oh, no, Cassie,' said Emily, shocked. 'We mustn't.'

'Well, *I'm* going,' said Cassie, thrusting her chin forward. 'I'm determined to find out if Miss Oakland's the thief.'

'I can't,' said Emily. 'I'm too scared.'

'Oh, come on, Em. It's safe. We saw her go out. As long as we're quick.'

Before Emily had a chance to hesitate further, Cassie grabbed her hand and pulled her across to the teacher's room.

They were struck immediately by the orderliness of Miss Oakland's belongings. Emily felt too nervous to touch anything.

'Keep watch at the door!' hissed Cassie, while she looked for Miss Oakland's jewellery box. Then she realised it was staring her in the face – a Chinese wooden box on top of a chest of drawers. She opened it and rummaged through the beads and brooches feverishly. Near the bottom she found the silver charm bracelet.

'Come and look, Emily!' she cried. She could hardly believe her eyes. There was an extra link dangling where a charm should have hung. She put it back and closed the lid, with trembling hands. Emily stared at her.

'Let's get out quick,' said Cassie.

But as they moved towards the door, Miss Oakland walked through it. She was as astonished as they were shocked.

'What are you doing in here?' she demanded.

'Oh, er, we were trying to find you, Miss Oakland,' said Cassie nervously.

'Well, you don't just walk in,' said the teacher. 'This is really very rude of you. I don't know what you were thinking of.'

'Sorry, Miss Oakland,' they said.

'What was it you wanted anyway?'

Cassie racked her brains. For once her imagination failed her. She looked at Emily helplessly, and Emily looked at her. There was a horrible silence.

'I see,' said Miss Oakland, with a frown. 'You girls have had the *cheek* to come into my room, knowing full well I was not here.' She looked very angry. 'I can't *think* what you were doing in here. But perhaps you would like to explain to Miss Wrench. Report to her office at eight-thirty tomorrow morning. Now straight back to your rooms!'

Cassie felt very guilty for getting Emily into trouble.

'I'm ever so sorry, Em,' she said, as they returned to their landing.

'What do you think Miss Wrench will do?' asked Emily in a small voice.

'I don't know, really,' said Cassie. 'I hope it's nothing too awful.'

The next morning, Becky was still feeling unwell. Cassie and Emily left her in the dining-hall once they'd eaten their breakfast, to report to Miss Wrench. They both felt very scared as they waited outside her office. They could hear Miss Oakland's voice through the door, though they couldn't make out her words.

'You don't think they'd ask us to leave, do you?' asked Emily.

'No, of course not,' said Cassie, trying to sound confident.

'Because I couldn't bear it now, not after getting the Allingham Bursary and everything.'

'It'll be all right, you'll see,' comforted Cassie.

At last they were asked to come in and Miss

Wrench sternly reprimanded them for going into Miss Oakland's room.

If only I could tell her Miss Oakland might be the thief of Petrakova's shoe, thought Cassie. *Then she'd think differently.*

Miss Wrench put them both in detention for a week but then Cassie had a further shock.

'Cassandra,' said Miss Wrench, 'Amanda Renwick has also reported to me that you attacked her quite viciously yesterday.'

Cassie hadn't expected Amanda to carry out her threat. Her heart sank. She was in deep trouble now.

'But, Miss Wrench, *she* attacked *me*. I only . . .'

'Lying won't help you one little bit,' Miss Wrench cut in. 'Amanda showed me a nasty bruise on her head that you'd given her.'

Cassie sighed. It was hopeless.

'I need hardly say that we don't expect such behaviour from our students at Redwood. I shall be asking Madame Larette to hold back your solo part for the time being. I'll make a final decision when I've had reports from all your teachers during the next week.'

Cassie left the office quite stunned. She had been so delighted that she was to dance a solo at the Gala performance. And now that chance might be taken away from her. It was Emily's turn to comfort her.

She went through ballet class that morning in a daze, performing the exercises quite mechanically. But ten minutes before break, Madame dismissed everyone except the few who had recently passed Grade Five. This small group gathered round her curiously.

'Now, *mes chéries*, I have a little surprise for you.'

From her small office, she brought out a box and placed it on the floor between them.

'Pointe shoes,' she explained, lifting up a pair of pink satin block-toed shoes. 'Take your shoes off.'

The girls stripped off their flat shoes and feverishly began trying on the new ones. Madame Larette made sure that each girl had the correct size and gave each a strip of elastic and a pair of pink ribbons.

'Take these to needlework this afternoon,' she instructed them, 'and Mrs White will show you how to darn the toes.'

'When shall we start using them?' Cassie asked, her eyes shining with excitement despite the awful morning she had had.

'Tomorrow, at the end of class, you will be 'aving five minutes. No more! Now, go!'

The girls scurried off, clutching their shoes, like new-found treasure.

But by the end of the morning, Cassie was feeling gloomy once more. Everything seemed to be going wrong. The three friends sat down to lunch, looking as miserable as donkeys on a beach.

Becky pushed her food round her plate. 'I don't fancy this,' she said.

'But it's your favourite!' cried Cassie. 'Sausage and mash!'

'I don't feel hungry either,' said Emily. 'Detention for a whole week. It's not fair.'

Becky stood up. 'I can't eat anything. I think I must have flu. I'm going to lie down for a while.'

'Why don't I take you to sick-bay?' suggested Cassie.

'No, I'll be all right after a rest. See you later.'

'She doesn't look very well, does she?' said Emily, when Becky had gone.

'No,' agreed Cassie. 'When Becky won't eat, she's got to be ill! Oh, why is everything going wrong at the moment?'

'Well, not quite everything.'

'I've got a great idea,' said Cassie. 'Let's pop over to see Mrs Allingham now. We haven't been for weeks.'

The idea of seeing their elderly friend was comforting.

'OK,' said Emily. 'We might as well use our freedom now, as all our free time after supper has been wiped out.'

Mrs Allingham was glad of their company and their help in the garden.

'You know girls,' she said, 'I've been thinking. You're getting busier at school as time goes by. I think I shall hire a gardener.'

'Good idea,' said Cassie. 'But may we still come and see you?'

'Of course you may,' said Mrs Allingham, beaming. 'You'll always be more than welcome at my door. Now, tell me all the Redwood news.'

Cassie intimated that she had been in trouble with Miss Wrench because of Amanda, but didn't go into details.

'Don't worry, dear, it'll all blow over. I remember what it's like with young girls falling out.'

Cassie knew it wasn't quite like that, but didn't argue. She didn't say anything about suspecting Miss Oakland of being the thief either. She knew Mrs Allingham wouldn't approve of their nosing around a teacher's room.

'Now come in for a drink. It's almost time for you to get back.'

The old lady led them into her small oak-beamed sitting-room, crammed with antiques, ornaments and frilly cushions. She poured out fruit juice. Cassie sank back into the comfortable sofa, sipping her drink.

'Do you know anything about Miss Oakland?' she asked.

'I've met her,' replied Mrs Allingham, 'but I don't know much about her, no. She's only been here a couple of years, but she's a very fine teacher, I hear.'

'She is good,' said Emily, 'but very strict.'

'Oh, I know what I've been meaning to tell you,' said Mrs Allingham. 'Do you remember asking me about Anna Petrokova's husband? Well, I was talking to Miss Wrench the other day, and I discovered from her that he's one of the trustees of the school.'

'How interesting! Did you find out his name?' asked Cassie.

'No, I didn't ask. Why? Is it important?' said Mrs Allingham.

'Probably not,' said Cassie, sighing.

As they waved goodbye to the old lady standing at her gate, Cassie reflected on the stupidity of her actions the night before. Now she had to face a week of detentions and the strong possibility that her sea-nymph solo would be taken away from her. How would she be able to explain it to Mrs Allingham, let alone her parents?

8

Sick-Bay

Cassie and Emily had to run the last few yards to school to be in time for registration after lunch. The lesson happened to be maths and when they sat down at their table, Cassie was surprised to see that Becky's place was empty.

'Rebecca Hastings?' called Miss Eiseldown.

Cassie put up her hand.

'Yes, Cassandra?'

'Miss Eiseldown, Becky was feeling ill at lunchtime and went to her room for a lie-down.'

'Oh, I see. Would you go along and see if she's all right, please? If necessary, take her to sick-bay. Matron can keep an eye on her then.'

'Yes, Miss Eiseldown.'

Cassie shot off down the corridor, slowing down only when she saw Miss Oakland in the distance. She took the stairs to her landing two at a time and burst into the bedroom.

The noise woke Becky, who was lying on her bed. 'Oh, I must have fallen asleep,' she said.

'It's maths now,' said Cassie. 'How do you feel?'

Becky slowly sat up. She looked very tired. 'I feel peculiar,' she said.

'How do you mean?'

'The room's swaying, and my throat hurts and I just feel I have to lie down.'

'I'm sure a nice chocolate biscuit would put you right,' said Cassie, fishing in her locker for one.

'No thanks,' said Becky. 'I feel a bit sick too.'

'Oh dear, it must be bad,' Cassie joked, but underneath she knew that Becky must really be feeling ill. Cassie got her a drink of water and went to fetch Matron, a timid little woman who was rarely seen outside the kitchens and sick-bay. She dithered around Becky and felt her forehead.

'You'd better come to sick-bay, dear,' she said finally. 'Cassie and I will give you a hand.'

Becky was feeling very dizzy by this time, so it wasn't an easy job helping her downstairs, but at last they had her tucked up in bed, with a white cotton hospital-type blanket as a coverlet. Cassie waited while Matron took her temperature.

'It's 103,' she announced. 'I think we'll have to call the doctor.'

'What's the matter with her?' asked Cassie anxiously.

'That's for the doctor to decide,' answered Matron. 'Now off you go back to your lesson. You can pop in to see Rebecca after supper.'

Cassie reported to Miss Eiseldown what had happened and tried to settle down to do some geometry. But her mind wouldn't stay on the subject for more than a few seconds.

'I'm worried about Becky,' Cassie whispered to Emily.

'Well, if the doctor's coming, she'll be in good hands.'

'I've just had a horrible thought,' said Cassie. 'I'll be on my own tonight with Amanda! I don't think I can stand it!'

'Come and share my bed,' said Emily. 'You did the same for me once, remember?'

'Oh, don't remind me! The ghost!'

'Do you think there really is one?' asked Emily.

'Yes, don't you? It must be the ghost of a dancer who used to come here. I'm sure she was wearing a ballet dress – I could see the net of the skirt.' Cassie looked thoughtful.

'Enough of ghosts — it's making my spine tingle. Are you going to see Becky later?'

'Yes, after supper,' said Cassie. 'Oh, no, I've got detention!'

Cassie managed to slip across to sick-bay during homework period in the end.

'How is she?' she asked Matron, who was just

leaving the patient, brandishing a thermometer.

'You can't go in there,' fussed the little woman. 'She's got measles. I had the doctor here earlier.'

'Measles!' cried Cassie. She hadn't thought of that. 'Oh, but it's all right, Matron. I've had them, when I was seven.'

'Well, if you're sure,' said Matron doubtfully. Cassie rushed past her, before she changed her mind.

Even though the room was darkened by the drawn curtains, Cassie could see the rash over Becky's face.

'Poor you!' she said. 'How do you feel?'

'Awful,' groaned Becky. 'I'm so hot, and yet shivery at the same time.'

'How could you desert me, Becky? Honestly!'

'Sorry,' said Becky, with a weak smile. 'I should ask Miss Eiseldown if Emily can have my bed while I'm out of action.'

'What a brill idea!' Cassie saw a look of unhappiness pass over Becky's face. 'But it won't be the same as having you there, Becky.'

'I've got to go home for a couple of weeks, when my temperature's come down. Matron's already phoned Mum.'

'Well, you'll probably enjoy that, when you start feeling a bit better.'

'Yes. At least it's a rest from boring ballet lessons.'

Cassie laughed. She couldn't understand Becky's attitude to dancing.

'Pour me a drink of water, will you, Cassie. I'm parched.'

Cassie filled a tumbler from the tap in the room and brought it back to her bedside.

'Can I bring you some books or magazines?'

'No, Matron said no reading. She says that I must have total rest.'

'You're going to be bored stiff!'

'You're telling me!'

'I know – you can borrow my Walkman. I haven't many tapes at school, but you can listen to what I've got.'

'Thanks.'

'I'd better go. It's a rehearsal with Madame. I'll bring you the Walkman first thing tomorrow.'

As Cassie rushed off to change into her leotard, a thought crossed her mind. What if that turned out to be the very last time she talked to Becky? She shook herself. Her imagination must be working overtime.

The next morning, Cassie bolted her breakfast and rushed down to sick-bay with her Walkman.

Becky's room was empty!

'Where's Becky?' Cassie asked, matron.

'I'm afraid Rebecca's very poorly and the doctor had her admitted to hospital late last night.'

'Oh, no!' groaned Cassie. 'I didn't think measles could be *that* serious.'

'I think there must be complications,' said Matron, in a confiding tone, as if that explained everything. 'But don't you worry, dear. She'll get the best care there is.'

Suddenly it was all too much. Cassie started to

cry. Matron sat her down on the bed and offered her a tissue. After a while, she patted Cassie's hand. 'Better now?'

'Yes thanks,' she sniffed and got up to leave. 'I'd better go,' she said. 'Ballet class!'

Madame took in Cassie's puffy eyes at once. She had heard that Rebecca had been rushed into hospital. She drew Cassie to one side, as the other girls took their places at the barre.

'I've had a word with Miss Wrench about your solo,' she said. 'And I've persuaded her to let you go ahead with it.'

'Oh, thank you, Madame!' Cassie cried. At least that was one thing that had turned out right.

At the end of class, Madame kept back the group who had passed Grade Five, for five minutes' pointe work. Six newly-darned pairs of pointe shoes were carefully put on, and six pairs of satin ribbons tied just so round the ankle. The girls rubbed their new shoes in the resin box and stood in first position, awaiting Madame's instructions.

She took them first to the barre, where she asked them to practise demi-plié, followed by a rise, in first position, on to full pointe. Cassie loved the feeling – a little like walking on stilts. Then Madame let them try echappés into second position, shooting their feet apart en pointe, then bringing them together again in demi-plié.

'À la seconde!' Madame reminded them, then off they went. The fairly simple exercise seemed so much more exciting on full pointe.

All too quickly their five minutes was over. Madame clapped her hands, and they offered her a curtsey, not without groans at the shortness of the practice.

'You will thank me later,' said their teacher. 'After bath tonight, you dab surgical spirit to your toes, *non*?'

'What's that for?' asked Emily, puzzled.

'Don't you know?' said Amanda. 'It hardens the skin.'

'Quite right, Amanda,' said Madame Larette. 'It 'ardens the skin of the toes. *Très bien, mes chéries*, another five minutes tomorrow.'

'Oh, why does it have to be so short?' moaned Cassie.

'We 'ave to be *so* careful,' Madame replied. 'Your feet, they are still growing. Much damage can be done to the joints, if the muscles are not strong and ready for this work. You are all the lucky ones, that your first teachers did not allow you en pointe too early. We see many girls 'ere at audition, whose feet are already ruined – and they are only ten years of age!'

Madame was growing quite heated. It was obviously a subject which concerned her a great deal.

'Now, *mes chéries*, you must do *exactement* what I tell you! *Cinq minutes* a day at first, no more!'

She had become so excited that she wouldn't even let them take their pointe shoes away with them, but locked them in her store cupboard, after they had each written their name inside their own pair.

As they walked along the corridor, Cassie and Emily heard Amanda and Sharon whispering behind them.

'Watch out,' said Emily. 'There's something brewing, I think.'

Their first lesson after break was Maths and Miss Eiseldown called the two girls over to her desk.

'We've just had news from the hospital,' she said.

'How's Becky?' asked Cassie, crossing her fingers fervently behind her back.

'Still not very well, I'm afraid. They've diagnosed viral meningitis. Rebecca's going to be in hospital for quite a while.'

'Isn't it terribly dangerous?' asked Cassie.

'It isn't the deadly sort of meningitis, and thankfully it's not at all infectious,' said Miss Eiseldown. 'Basically, it's an inflammation – of the lining of the brain.'

'Oh, it sounds horrible!' cried Emily. 'Poor Becky.'

'Don't worry now, girls,' said Miss Eiseldown kindly. 'She's getting the best care. When she's feeling a bit better, she'll be transferred to the hospital in her home-town, so her parents can be with her as much as they like.'

'I can't believe it!' said Cassie. 'She's always been so lively and full of fun.'

'Look,' said Miss Eiseldown, 'as her housemother, I'm keeping in touch with the hospital and Mr and

Mrs Hastings, so as soon as there's any improvement, I'll let you know.'

'Thank you, Miss Eiseldown,' said Cassie. 'Oh, I nearly forgot, would it be all right if Emily moved in with me while Becky's away?'

Miss Eiseldown knew all about the trouble between Amanda and Cassie. She nodded. 'Yes, in the circumstances, I'll allow you to do that.'

After this conversation, Cassie just kept thinking of Becky's cheerful face, as she had seen her last in sick-bay. How she wished she could visit her in hospital! But perhaps Becky would be too ill to speak to her. She couldn't bear that.

In the lunch-hour, she was sitting on a log outside with Emily in the sunshine, when Sharon came running up to her.

'Mr Green says you're to go to the music room immediately,' she commanded. Sharon was obviously enjoying her errand.

'Oh, no!' cried Cassie, jumping up. 'I've forgotten my violin lesson.'

She raced to her room for her violin and rushed across school to the music room. Mr Green looked cross. 'We have only five minutes left, Cassandra. Don't let this happen again, please.'

'No, sorry, Mr Green.'

'Just play me the new Grade Three piece we went over last week.'

After quickly tuning up, and finding the correct music, Cassie attempted the piece. She played it badly and guessed what was coming next.

'More practice, Cassandra. This won't do. Your examination is not very far away. If you don't pull your socks up, you won't be entered for it.'

The sharpness in Mr Green's voice was enough to make Cassie burst into tears.

'Now now, don't take it so hard,' said the amazed violin teacher.

'It's not you,' sobbed Cassie. 'It's Becky.'

He couldn't get any more sense out of her before his next pupil arrived. Cassie recovered herself as best she could and took her violin back to her room.

Over the next few days, there was no change in Becky's condition – the hospital was still saying she was very poorly. Cassie had lost all interest in the theft of Petrakova's ballet shoe. She had told Becky of course about the missing charm on Miss Oakland's bracelet, but the little ballerina still remained locked away in Becky's jewellery box, and Cassie had neither the enthusiasm nor the energy to do anything else about it.

The one thing that kept her going was her dancing. Madame Larette had begun to teach her and Emily their nymph solos. And, after each morning class, they had the joy of five minutes' pointe work practice.

Friday was no exception. The small group of girls gathered around the box of block-toed shoes Madame had kept locked in her cupboard. She still suspected that they would be tempted to practise in their rooms if they were allowed to keep their shoes.

They went through the set of exercises Madame had shown them at the barre. When Cassie began her échappés she began to feel a strange tingling in her toes.

'More surgical spirit tonight,' she told herself. At the end of the exercise, she looked round and saw Emily rubbing one of her feet. Then the soles of Cassie's feet began to burn and itch! She and Emily exchanged looks and groaned. They both sat down, tore off their new ballet shoes and scratched their toes and feet for all they were worth.

Madame stared at them in astonishment.

'Sorry, Madame,' panted Cassie, 'but I think someone's put itching powder in our shoes.' She stared accusingly at Amanda, but Amanda was wide-eyed, as if surprised.

'Nonsense!' cried Madame Larette. 'Your shoes 'ave been locked up all night.'

She dismissed the group of girls and reluctantly allowed them their shoes to take home for half-term, first making them promise that they would only wear them for ten minutes each day, and would only practise the strengthening exercises she had taught them. Then she advised Cassie and Emily – still scratching furiously – to go to sick-bay, to see if they had something infectious.

When they found Matron, she made them both wash their feet and inspected them carefully.

'It looks like an allergy to me,' she said. 'But it's funny you've both got it at the same time.'

'We think it's itching powder,' said Cassie.

Matron ran a finger inside one of the shoes and found a trace of powder.

'Looks like you may be right,' she agreed. She gave them some calamine lotion to soothe the itching and said she would report the incident to Miss Eiseldown.

'Well at least someone believes us,' Emily said to Cassie as they left sick-bay.

'Yes, but goodness knows how anyone got hold of the shoes when they were locked away the whole time in Madame's cupboard.'

'Unless it was the ghost,' said Emily, with a shudder.

'Do ghosts play practical jokes?' asked Cassie.

The girls were still puzzling over this new mystery at half past six, as they packed their bags for the forthcoming half-term holiday.

9

Half-Term Outings

Jake Brown was taken aback when Cassie rushed into his arms outside the main door.

'Whatever's the matter, Cassie?' he asked, after she'd nearly squeezed the breath out of him.

'It's Becky, Dad,' Cassie blurted out. 'She had measles and the doctor sent her to hospital and now she's got an inflammation and I'm really worried about her.'

Sitting beside her dad in the car, Cassie poured out all her troubles. Jake did his best to raise her spirits and once they were home, the first thing he did was to phone Becky's parents.

'What did they say?' Cassie asked eagerly, when

he returned to the sitting-room.

'I spoke to her father. Her mum's at the hospital in Birmingham. He said she was a little better, and they're transferring her tomorrow.'

'Will she be all right, do you think?' Cassie asked in a small voice.

'Yes, it's dangerous, but I'm sure she'll pull through.'

Joy put her arms around Cassie and gave her a generous hug. 'Don't worry, love. Becky's such a lively girl. She'll bounce back.'

Cassie didn't feel like watching television with her parents and Adam, and said she was going to have an early night. She got into bed, but wasn't really tired, so she sat up reading until well after her bedtime.

At ten o'clock, her mum came in to see her. 'How are you feeling?'

'Bit better.'

'Daddy and I thought you needed something to cheer you up, so we've arranged a treat for tomorrow night.'

'What is it?' Cassie asked, her eyes lighting up.

'Wait and see,' said Joy. 'It's a surprise.'

Her mother would say no more the next day, but at tea-time, which was unusually early, she explained to Adam and Rachel that she was taking Cassie out and that they were to be good. She asked Cassie to put on her best dress and at six o'clock, they left for their secret destination.

Joy drove down the motorway and then followed signs for the city centre.

'It looks like you're taking me back to school!' Cassie exclaimed.

'Have another guess,' said Joy.

'Are we going to the theatre?'

'You've got it,' laughed her mother. She managed to park in a multi-storey carpark quite near to the theatre.

'The performance starts at seven-fifteen, so we've quarter of an hour to pick up our tickets and buy a programme.'

As they rounded the corner, Cassie saw the Hippodrome in front of her, and a large poster advertising the Bolshoi Ballet.

'Oh, that's wonderful, Mum!' cried Cassie. 'I've always wanted to see Russian dancers.'

'Well, now's your chance. They're dancing *Giselle* tonight.'

Cassie could hardly believe her ears. Her very favourite ballet!

From the moment the curtains parted until they closed, she was transported to another world – the world of the simple peasant girl, Giselle, who falls in love with Albrecht, a nobleman in disguise. When his real fiancée comes into the village, his identity is revealed, and Giselle goes mad and dies, very dramatically, of a broken heart.

Act Two is set in the graveyard in which Giselle is buried. Cassie's mother began to wonder if the ballet had been a good choice after all, but Cassie seemed to be completely absorbed in it. The Wilis filled the stage with graceful, fluttering movements

– they were the spirits of girls who had been betrayed by men. And then came the nerve-tingling moment when the Queen of the Wilis calls up Giselle's spirit from her grave to dance with them. The two leading female roles stood in great contrast: Giselle, soft and ethereal, the Queen, brittle and commanding.

Albrecht brings flowers to Giselle's grave and the Queen of the Wilis orders Giselle to dance him to his death. Reluctantly, she obeys, and dances with him, but returns to her grave before dawn, so that he can live. Left alone at the end, Albrecht lies grief-stricken on the stage.

Cassie gave her nose a good blow.

'That was the most wonderful thing I've ever seen!' she said.

'I was a bit worried that it was going to be too sad for you,' said Joy, looking at her daughter with concern.

'Oh, no,' replied Cassie. 'It's made me feel sort of washed new, if you know what I mean.'

When they reached home, Jake had fallen asleep in his armchair. Cassie woke him up to tell him about *Giselle*.

'I can't wait to tell Madame Larette that I've seen the Bolshoi,' she said, when she kissed her parents goodnight.

Later she dreamed that she was dancing in a ballet like *Giselle*, only it was Becky's grave and she was bringing flowers to it. Then a ghost rose from the grave, and she felt terrified, even though she was still dancing. The nightmare woke her up around dawn and from then on she lay awake thinking about Becky, until she heard her parents stirring in the kitchen downstairs.

Cassie spent a quiet Sunday, which gave her time to calm down after the upsets and excitements of the previous week. On Monday, she was allowed to phone Becky's house. Her mother answered.

'Hello, Mrs Hastings. It's Cassie here. How's Becky?'

'Well, much better, thank you. She's been chattering to me all day, and she managed to walk a bit with a little help.'

'That's wonderful,' said Cassie.

'Look, Cassie, would your parents run you over here? I know Becky would love to see you.'

'Yes, I'm sure they would!'

'If they could bring you on Thursday morning, I'll take you with me to visit her after lunch, and we could go again in the evening. You could stay the night with us, to save your parents having to do both journeys in one day.'

'I'll just check with Mum.' After a quick conversation with Joy, Cassie hurried back to the phone. 'Yes, she says that's fine.'

'Great,' said Mrs Hastings. 'I know it'll cheer Becky up no end.'

Cassie asked her mum to stop in town on their way to the Hastings' on Thursday. She wanted to buy Becky a present, and after looking round several shops, decided on a watercolour set and pad.

It took them an hour and a half to reach Gloucester and another fifteen minutes to find Becky's house. Mrs Hastings made Cassie feel at home straight away. It was odd seeing Becky's house for the first time without Becky in it, and even more so when Mrs Hastings took her up to Becky's room.

'I'll leave you here to settle in, while I make your mother a cup of coffee,' she said, which Cassie took as a hint that she wanted to talk to her mum in private.

She laid her nightdress on Becky's bed and spent a few minutes looking at her posters, tapes and books. The posters and tapes were no surprise – Cassie knew which stars Becky liked. But her book collection was vastly different from Cassie's: there was no fiction. All Becky's books were factual and most were about the workings of the human body, or animal and insect life.

'A vet in the making!' Cassie thought to herself. Then she had a pang of anxiety, wondering if Becky's brain had been at all damaged by her illness.

Mrs Hastings called her down for a glass of juice, so she shook off that disagreeable thought and joined them in the sitting-room.

'I was just telling your mother,' said Mrs Hastings gently, 'that it is unlikely that Becky will ever come back to Redwood.'

Cassie had expected this. 'I shall miss her a lot,' she said simply.

Mrs Hastings' eyes filled with tears as she explained it would be a long time before Becky regained full co-ordination, so that a ballet training looked out of the question.

'Poor Rebecca,' she sighed. 'It's so disappointing for her.'

'Well, perhaps she won't take it too badly,' said Cassie.

'No, Becky was made to be a ballerina,' said Mrs Hastings. 'It has been a tragic blow for her.'

Cassie opened her mouth to argue but caught a warning look from Joy. Then she remembered how often Becky had tried to convince her mother that she disliked ballet. She had failed every time, so it was unlikely anything Cassie said would have any effect.

After lunch, Mr and Mrs Hastings drove Cassie to the hospital. Becky was their only child and it was clear that Mrs Hastings doted on her daughter.

Cassie's nervousness about visiting Becky soon vanished when she actually saw her. It was the same old cheeky grin, even though her face had lost its roundness.

'Hi, Cassie,' she cried cheerfully.

'Hi, Becky,' said Cassie, thrusting the tissue-wrapped present under her nose. 'I've brought you something to keep you busy.'

'Oh, that's a lovely idea!' said Becky when she had unwrapped the present. 'I'll paint all the nurses and the other kids in the ward.'

Cassie laughed. She was so pleased that Becky

seemed all right. Mr and Mrs Hastings went off to do some shopping, leaving the girls together 'for a gossip', as they put it. Cassie filled her in on all the Redwood news, making the most out of the itching-powder incident. And Becky gave Cassie the run-down on all the other children in the ward, and some of the sad and funny things that were wrong with them.

'That gorgeous boy over there,' she whispered to her friend. 'He's fourteen and he's in with a broken leg. And guess how he did it?'

'How?'

'Falling down his front door-step!'

Cassie chuckled.

Becky paused and looked thoughtful. 'You know I'm not coming back, don't you?'

'Yes, but . . .' said Cassie, feeling uncomfortable.

'Oh, don't worry. Mum hasn't told me yet, but I can put two and two together all right.'

'Do you mind, Becky?'

'No. I shan't miss the dancing. I'll be able to do more Maths and Science at our local school. But I'll miss you and Emily.'

'We'll try and see each other every holiday!' Cassie said. 'I'm sure Mum and Dad will let you stay with me whenever you want.'

Becky's eyes lit up. 'That would be great. And you must come and stay with me,' she said. 'By the way, my dad's coming down to collect my clothes and things next Tuesday.' She lowered her voice to a whisper. 'I've been worrying about the silver ballerina. It's still in my jewellery box. It had better not come home in case Mum and Dad find it.'

'No, of course. But how can I get it out? You locked the box, remember?'

'The key's in the top drawer of my chest, inside a black and white striped sock.'

Cassie promised she would remove the charm from Becky's jewellery box and it wasn't mentioned again that afternoon, as Mr and Mrs Hastings returned from shopping quite soon after, and during their evening visit they stayed with the girls the whole time.

The short stay with the Hastings was rather clouded by Becky's request. It kept coming back to Cassie's mind, like a catchy tune, and she began to wish she had never seen the silver ballerina.

10

Imprisoned

As Sunday evening approached, Cassie became more and more apprehensive about returning to Redwood. She knew how much she would miss Becky, and there was uncertainty about how long Emily would be able to stay with her.

After the hour's drive there with her dad, she was delighted to find Emily and Jane already in her room, and that Amanda was nowhere in sight.

She kissed her dad goodbye and talked almost non-stop to her friends for the next hour, about *Giselle* and her visit to Becky.

'Did she seem very ill?' asked Emily.

'She's pretty bright really, but she can hardly walk

105

still. Her mum says it'll be ages before her co-ordination's back to normal.'

'Isn't she coming back to Redwood then?'

'No, I don't think so. Isn't it awful?'

'Poor Becky,' sighed Emily. 'And I thought *I* was the one who was going to have to leave.'

'I suppose none of us is safe really,' said Cassie thoughtfully.

'Amanda's late tonight,' Emily commented.

'She often is,' said Cassie, 'and her parents never come up to the room with her. Apart from the very first day, when her dad was with her.'

'What about her mother?'

'No, never.'

Cassie suddenly had one of her 'good ideas'. 'Why don't we play detectives and see if we can spot her arriving? We might get a look at her parents.'

'I'll leave you to it,' said Jane. 'I haven't finished unpacking yet.'

Cassie and Emily put on their outdoor shoes and jumpers and slipped out into the garden. Working their way quietly round the building, they ended up behind the shrubbery at one side of the front drive.

'This'll do,' said Cassie. 'We can see, but can't be seen.'

Several girls arrived, but no Amanda. Then, after ten minutes or so of waiting, a white Mercedes drew up into the car park with a uniformed driver. He opened the back door, and helped Amanda out.

Cassie and Emily stared at one another. 'I knew she was rich,' said Cassie, 'but not *that* rich!'

106

'That's why we never see her parents,' said Emily.

Amanda walked through the large oak front doors, carrying her luggage, and the Mercedes swept away down the drive.

The two girls retraced their steps but decided to visit Jane in Emily's old room in order to avoid Amanda until bedtime. Cassie still more than half suspected it was Amanda who had put itching powder in their pointe shoes. If only she could work out how she'd done it!

The rising bell the following morning seemed monstrously early. All three girls had got used to lying in bed late at home. Amanda was the first up, while Cassie and Emily turned over and had another ten minutes in bed. When they had woken themselves properly by splashing cold water on their faces, they had to change into their pink leotards, tights and red track suits at breakneck speed. Chatting to each other nineteen to the dozen, they quickly plaited their hair, winding the two plaits around their heads and securing the ends with hair-grips.

'I'll be glad when we're third years,' said Emily.

'Why?'

'They have buns, not plaits.'

'Sounds even trickier to me!'

'How long do we have the *pleasure* of your company?' Amanda suddenly asked Emily.

'I'm not sure,' replied Emily. 'Probably as long as Becky's away.'

Amanda made no reply but it was clear by the

look on her face that she wasn't too pleased at the news. On their way to ballet class, Cassie told Emily that she had to get the silver ballerina from Becky's jewellery box before the next day.

'It's a pity Jane was in the room yesterday. Let's hope Amanda doesn't stay in our room all evening,' said Cassie.

'Or you might manage it in the lunch-hour,' suggested Emily. 'I still think you should have handed it in long ago.'

'Oh, I don't know *what* to do with it now. I can't ask Miss Oakland point blank, because if she is the thief, she'll simply deny it's hers, won't she?'

'Give it to Miss Wrench. Say you found it this morning.'

'But she'll never believe me, Em.'

Emily shrugged. 'It's up to you.'

Miss Oakland was taking ballet class, while Madame Larette was busy preparing a group of second years for an exam. All went smoothly until they came to their échappés sautées in the centre. She made the whole class repeat this exercise again and again.

'No, no!' she cried out in exasperation. 'You look like so many Mr Plods! Take your sautée upwards first, *before* you jump outwards into second.'

The exercise was done again.

'What about your arms?' she shouted. 'If you are still travelling *upwards*, why are your arms going out to second? Echo what your legs are doing with your arms. Let me see you, three at a time. First I'll have Emily, Cassandra and Jane. Ready, and . . .'

Although Cassie was weary of repeating the échappés so often, she was surprised what a difference Miss Oakland's advice made. She was able to get much greater elevation, and land more gracefully too.

'That's it, Cassandra,' said Miss Oakland. 'Thank goodness *someone's* been listening.'

Cassie felt a glow of pleasure. To be praised by Miss Oakland was really something. The next three were Amanda, Sharon and Sandra. Amanda executed her échappés with polish, but without the height that Cassie had achieved. But Miss Oakland's hawk-like eyes had been fastened on Sharon.

'Disgusting!' cried the teacher. 'Your rear end was sticking right out when you landed. Horrible! Do it again!'

Sharon tried again, but with little improvement. 'I can't bear to watch you!' shouted Miss Oakland. 'This isn't Redwood standard at all.'

Cassie wondered if she had forgotten Sharon was leaving at the end of term. The next moment, Sharon was in floods of tears.

'Stop snivelling, you silly girl,' said Miss Oakland. 'You're big enough and daft enough to take a bit of criticism.'

Cassie's heart went out to Sharon, even though she disliked her. Sharon, still crying, rushed out of the studio to the changing-room. Miss Oakland looked annoyed.

'Let's have your curtsey, girls. It's almost time to

109

finish. I want the pre-elementary group to stay behind for a few minutes' pointe work practice.'

After their curtsey, Miss Oakland held up her hand. 'Before the rest of you disappear, I've got something to ask you all. Has anyone found a silver charm? I seem to have lost one from my charm bracelet.'

Emily looked at Cassie. Cassie felt a blush rising from her toes. What should she do? While she was still deciding, Jane put up her hand.

'Yes, Jane?'

'What kind of charm is it, Miss Oakland?'

'It's a little monkey. Have any of you seen it?'

In the silence which followed Cassie could almost hear Emily's surprise.

'OK then. Off you go girls. Apart from the pointe work group.'

Cassie stood, astonished. She wasn't too sorry that the ballet teacher was no longer chief suspect – but what was she to do about the silver ballerina? Who on earth did it belong to?

While pondering this, she attacked her pointe work with great energy. Her toes and feet felt much stronger now and she was able for the first time to balance on one tiptoe, although this felt pretty uncomfortable. At the end of the lesson, she took off her shoes and looked at them. Despite all the darning, the satin had already begun to wear in places. She massaged her feet. Emily sat down on the floor of the changing-room with her.

'So it isn't Miss Oakland,' she whispered.

'No,' breathed Cassie. 'We've got to think again. But first, we've got to get that charm out of Becky's box.'

'I've got netball practice – I'd forgotten. How about you?'

'Music lesson. But I might get the chance when I go up for my violin.'

When Cassie nipped into her room at lunch-time, she found Amanda there already, changing for netball. Her opportunity lost, she went straight to the music room. Having managed to fit in a couple of decent violin practices at home after her return from Gloucester, she was able to go along to Mr Green with much more confidence. She played her Grade Three pieces quite fluently and the music teacher told her he was pleased with her. Cassie thought to herself that he probably wouldn't dare speak sharply to her ever again, in case she burst out crying!

Miss Eiseldown saw Cassie and Emily after lunch and told them that Emily could officially stay in Cassie's room until the end of term.

'Becky's father is coming to collect her things tomorrow, I believe, so you'll be able to move in properly, then, Emily.'

Cassie's next chance to retrieve the ballerina came when afternoon school was over. She and Emily raced back to their room, hoping that Amanda might go and join Sharon and Sandra for the homework period, as she sometimes did. But their hopes were dashed, when Amanda followed quite quickly and settled down at her desk to do some homework. The two friends could think of nothing better than to follow suit.

Soon it was time to hang up their school uniform for the day. The red cardigans and grey kilts came off; their purple leotards and leggings went on. Plaits were wound round heads again and track suits and modern dance pumps donned.

Mrs Bonsing took them for an energetic hour's lesson in jazz and ballet. Cassie often didn't like the music chosen for these dance classes, but today it was television themes, which all the students recognised. The boys joined in with this class and during a couple of rests, Cassie was able to watch Matthew. He was a natural dancer, and in his element in the lively jazz sequence that Mrs Bonsing was teaching them.

After tea, Cassie and Emily rushed up to their bedroom, only to find that Amanda had beaten them to it. She had brought Sharon and Sandra with her to listen to her latest tape. As there was a rehearsal that evening, the girls tidied their hair, collected their ballet shoes and set off for the studio, with Amanda not far behind them.

Madame Larette told them she was going to teach them their solos for the Gala during the second half of the rehearsal. After the initial group work on the underwater ballet, Miss Waters, the new assistant ballet mistress, took over the rest of the class, while Madame led Cassie and Emily to one of the larger bedrooms. It was left uncarpeted and unfurnished, so that it could be used from time to time as an extra practice room. The girls had never been in it before.

There was no piano, but a tape recorder sat in one corner. Madame put on a recording of *The Planets* and found the track she wanted, 'Uranus', which was to be the music for their dance.

The dance began together – interweaving arms, bodies and legs. But then the nymph Nerine (played by Cassie) fell asleep in the middle of the stage, while Ursula moved around her in an undulating, graceful dance. About halfway through the piece of music, Ursula had to run off-stage, which was Nerine's signal to wake up. Then Cassie had a beautiful dreamy solo, which she thought matched the mood of the music perfectly.

'That's all we 'ave time for now,' said Madame Larette. 'I'm very pleased with the way you 'ave picked up the dance so far. Well done, *mes chéries*.'

Back in the changing-room, the girls couldn't help noticing that Amanda looked extremely cross.

'Of all the cheek!' Amanda exploded to Sharon and Sandra. 'Leaving us with Miss Waters – she's wet all right! I shall get my father to complain to Miss Wrench. We're supposed to have top-class tuition. Miss Waters ought to be teaching the pre-primary class at her local ballet school.' She broke off in a fit of coughing.

Cassie and Emily exchanged looks. Amanda seemed to hold a lot of sway with Miss Wrench – would Miss Waters last long at Redwood, they both wondered? They changed quickly and set off for

113

their room ahead of Amanda, but some sixth sense seemed to prompt Amanda to hurry after them, still coughing loudly. Cassie sighed inwardly. Here she was, at bedtime, with Amanda still very much in evidence, and the silver ballerina still locked away in Becky's jewellery box.

She decided before going to sleep to set her alarm for six o'clock. Amanda would still be fast asleep at that early hour. In the strange way that the mind sometimes works, Cassie woke the following morning exactly one minute before the alarm was due to go off. This was a stroke of luck – no danger now of the bleeping waking Amanda. She didn't bother to wake Emily, thinking to herself that one person padding about the room would certainly make less noise than two.

Cassie moved as slowly and quietly as she possibly could. The hardest part was pulling drawers open without making much noise. The small top drawer wasn't too bad – it ran easily on its runners and she soon spotted the striped black and white sock which housed the key. But the bottom drawer, where Becky kept the box itself, was more tricky. It was much stiffer and squeaked quite a lot while she was edging it open. With her heart in her mouth, she took out the box and inserted the key. The lid flipped open, and she quickly retrieved the silver ballerina from under a pile of bangles and badges.

Amanda turned over in bed. Cassie held her breath, but all went quiet again. Still clutching the charm, she returned the box and key to the bottom drawer and tried to close it as quietly as she could.

She was concentrating so hard on this difficult task, that Amanda's voice right behind her made her jump.

'What did you just take out of Becky's little box?' she demanded.

Cassie searched her mind for an explanation.

'Oh . . . er . . . just something Becky said I could have last weekend.'

'Let me see!' Amanda said, imperiously. By now Emily was awake and quickly guessed what must be happening.

'Leave her alone, Amanda,' she broke in. 'You know Becky's her best friend.'

'Open your hand,' cried Amanda, seizing it and trying to wrench Cassie's fingers open.

'Ow! You're hurting!' cried Cassie.

Desperately, Cassie tried to push Amanda's arm away, but Amanda wouldn't let go. As the two girls grappled, the door opened and Miss Eiseldown walked in.

'What's this commotion?' she asked.

Her words stopped the girls in their tracks. Cassie dropped the charm as Amanda released her hand. Both girls stared down at it.

'What's all this about?' asked Miss Eiseldown. 'I'm very disappointed to find you two fighting again.'

'She was trying to get the ballerina from me,' explained Cassie.

'But ask her where *she* got it from!' broke in Amanda, with a sudden glint in her eye.

115

'Well?' demanded the housemother.

Cassie hung her head. It was going to be terribly difficult to explain.

'I think we'd better postpone explanations until we get to Miss Wrench's office. Amanda, Cassandra, meet me there at eight.'

As Cassie suspected she would, Miss Wrench gave Amanda first opportunity to describe her version of events. A thought crossed her mind like a thunderbolt. What if she were expelled for stealing? Why on earth hadn't she taken Emily's advice and handed the charm to Miss Wrench?

Cassie had already made up her mind not to tell the whole story, and so when Miss Wrench tackled her, she was ready with an answer.

'You were caught red-handed, girl, stealing, I repeat, *stealing*, from a so-called friend's jewellery box. Quite despicable. What have you got to say for yourself? Eh?'

'I know it l-looks bad, Miss Wrench,' Cassie stammered, 'but I had Becky's permission to take the silver charm out of her box. She asked me to keep it for her.'

'A flagrant liar too!' thundered Miss Wrench. 'If Rebecca had wanted to give you something, she had every opportunity. And why should you choose six o'clock in the morning to go sneaking among her things, if you had her permission?'

Cassie racked her brains, but could find no satisfactory answer. Oh, if only she had handed in the wretched thing straight away!

116

'And what makes all this ten times worse is the fact that not long ago you were caught snooping around Miss Oakland's room! I have no alternative but to suspend you, Cassandra Brown.'

Miss Wrench poured more abuse on her head, but by now Cassie's mind had reached a far away place where the individual words didn't reach. She was only conscious of the noise, and of Amanda's face, flushed with triumph. When she came to, she was surprised to find Miss Eiseldown speaking quietly.

' . . . never shown any dishonesty beforehand and perhaps it would be wise to check out Cassie's story by asking Rebecca herself.'

A glimmer of hope shone in Cassie's eyes as she looked across at Miss Wrench.

'Oh, very well. I shall contact Mr and Mrs Hastings by telephone later. But I'm sure it will be a waste of time.'

Cassie's mind raced. Oh, no! If she only spoke to Becky's parents, they would know nothing about a silver charm!

'Until further notice, Cassandra, you will stay in your room. I shall have your meals sent up to you. You're dismissed.'

As she left the room, she heard Miss Wrench thanking Amanda for her prompt action.

Cassie felt sick. She hurried back to Emily, hoping that Amanda wouldn't follow her just yet. Once in her room, she threw herself on the bed and burst into bitter tears. Luckily Amanda didn't return until

117

after Cassie had composed herself and had had the chance to tell Emily about the interview.

Amanda came with Cassie's breakfast on a tray. *Like a jailer,* thought Cassie.

'Well, look where your temper's landed you now,' she said, sniffing.

'You're a busybody, Amanda,' said Cassie. 'Poking your nose in other people's business.'

'Yes,' added Emily. 'Becky did say Cassie could have that charm.'

'Miss Wrench didn't seem to agree, did she?' said Amanda sweetly.

Cassie asked Emily to return the tray of food to the dining-room. She couldn't face breakfast. She was just longing for Amanda to leave the room and leave her in peace.

As if guessing her thoughts, Amanda seemed to take twice as long as usual to get her books and equipment ready for the day's lessons. She still looked flushed and her eyes glittered strangely.

Cassie wondered to herself why Amanda was so pleased to get her into trouble. Was it just rivalry, or was there more to it than that?

As last she was left alone with Emily.

'Will you be all right on your own, Cassie?'

'Yes, much better without you-know-who,' Cassie replied.

'I'll come and see you in all the breaks,' Emily promised. 'And don't worry. Becky will put you in the clear, just as soon as she can speak to Miss Wrench.'

11

The Ghost Returns

As things turned out, it was Miss Eiseldown, not
Emily, who was first to visit Cassie in the lunch-
hour.

'Hello,' she said kindly. 'Not too miserable, I
hope.'

She smoothed her pretty floral, cotton skirt
under her and sat on Cassie's bed, beside her.

'I'm not a thief, Miss Eiseldown.'

'No, of course not,' she said soothingly. 'I've come
to let you know what's been happening. Miss
Wrench has been in touch with Rebecca's parents.
Unfortunately . . .' she sighed, 'they know nothing
of a silver charm. In fact they are adamant that

Rebecca has never owned a charm bracelet of any description.'

It was just as Cassie had feared.

'So,' went on Miss Eiseldown, 'the mystery deepens. At least until Mr and Mrs Hastings can talk to Rebecca about it at visiting time. There isn't anything else *you* want to tell me, is there, Cassie?'

Cassie shook her head. Her housemother sighed and stood up. 'I'm afraid you still have to stay in your room. By the way, Amanda has been given permission to move in with Sharon and Sandra. I think it will be better for everyone.'

Cassie smiled her agreement. Miss Eiseldown stood up.

'I sincerely hope that this whole business will be sorted out by this evening.'

Cassie thanked Miss Eiseldown and said goodbye to her. Only thirty seconds later, Emily burst into the room, carrying Cassie's lunch.

'You make a better jailer than Amanda anyway.'

'Glad to see you've got your sense of humour back,' said Emily, smiling.

Emily's visits were little rays of sunshine in a very bleak day, which seemed to drag on mercilessly. The afternoon was so boring that she got into bed. It was comforting, snuggled up under her quilt and in a surprisingly short time she was fast asleep.

She was woken by Emily. Classes had finished for the day and she had brought Matthew to see her. Cassie dressed quickly, as it was dangerous for him to be left out in the corridor for too long. Emily smuggled him in and the three of them sat on the floor. Matthew cheered Cassie up instantly.

He was doing a wonderful impersonation of Amanda, when Amanda herself walked in to collect her belongings. She barely spoke to them, which was a relief, but the atmosphere was tense and they all breathed a sigh of relief when she left.

Suddenly, there was a knock on the door. Matthew dived under Cassie's bed, as she went to answer it.

It was Miss Eiseldown. She looked around the room inquiringly. 'Glad to see you're keeping your spirits up, Cassie. I could have sworn I heard . . . Well, never mind.'

'Has Miss Wrench heard anything from the Hastings yet?' Cassie asked her eagerly.

'Yes. She made another telephone call a few minutes ago. Bad news, I'm afraid. Rebecca's had a relapse.'

'Oh, no!' cried Cassie. She could hardly believe so many bad things could happen all at once.

'She is conscious, but of course, her parents don't want to bother her with any questions while she's so poorly.'

'Do you think she'll get better?' asked Emily.

'Oh, I think the doctors still have high hopes. But it is a setback and must be very worrying for poor Rebecca's parents.'

'I must write her a letter,' said Cassie.

'I'm afraid,' went on Miss Eiseldown, 'that you

121

must stay in your room until this matter has been cleared up.'

'But that could take ages, now Becky's too ill to talk,' Emily blurted out.

'There's nothing I can do about it,' sighed the young teacher. 'Let's just hope and pray for everybody's sake that Rebecca will rally quickly. Now I really must go and prepare for my afternoon lessons.'

When the housemother's footsteps had died away, Matthew hauled himself out of his hiding-place.

'I thought she was never going to go!' he complained. 'It was suffocating under there.'

'You think *you've* got problems,' said Emily.

He turned to Cassie. 'I really am sorry, Casablanca. But it'll all turn out right for you in the end. I just know it will.'

'I think you'd better go now, Matthew,' urged Emily. 'If Amanda comes back and you're still here, she might decide to pay another visit to the Wrench and we've got troubles enough, I think.'

Because she had slept during the day, it took Cassie ages to fall asleep that night. Then, in the early hours of the morning, she woke with a start. Was she having a recurring dream? Or was she truly awake? For she could hear once again that soft padding along the landing. And, just as before, the slight rattle of the brass doorknob as it slowly turned.

Her heart thumping now, she forced herself to

lean over to Emily and shake her awake. As Emily opened her eyes in bewilderment, the door creaked open. The slender white hand, and the long pale fingers of Cassie's dream were clearly visible.

They were followed by a slim white arm. Then the door stood wide open, and both girls gasped in horror at what was now revealed.

Moonlight shimmered on the calf-length, white, net skirt and satin bodice of the *Giselle* costume they had stared at so many times in the entrance hall. Only this time it wasn't in a picture. Here was the portrait come to life! The dark-haired, graceful head of Petrakova was downcast, but the hand, the long pale finger, was pointing, pointing once again at Cassie.

Shutting her eyes tightly in terror, Cassie opened her mouth to scream, but no sound came out. Her legs and arms trembled with fright, and she felt cold and clammy. Then she heard several piercing screams, but was unable to tell if they were hers or Emily's, or a mixture.

'Has it gone do you think?' she whispered.

'I don't know,' said Emily. 'You look!'

'No, you!' said Cassie.

When they dared to open their eyes again they saw, not the ghost standing in the doorway, but Miss Eiseldown, running into the room.

'Whatever's happened?' she cried, switching on the light.

The girls both began talking hysterically about what they had seen. It was several minutes before

Miss Eiseldown understood them fully.

'And you say this ghost looked just like the picture of Petrakova?'

'Yes, yes, just like it!' cried Cassie.

Miss Eiseldown looked shaken. She sat down on Amanda's empty bed. 'I think I'd better stay here with you until morning.'

'Oh, thank you, Miss Eiseldown,' said Emily, looking relieved.

'Well, I don't think you'll get much sleep otherwise. Do you want me to leave the light on?'

'Yes, please!' chorused the two girls.

Cassie tossed and turned for a couple of hours. She couldn't get the ghost out of her head. She realised she must have fallen back to sleep when she was woken again by noises on the landing. Miss Eiseldown had obviously heard them too, as she was sitting up.

'Stay where you are,' she whispered to Cassie, slipping off Amanda's bed. She opened the door. It was Amanda, reeling around in her pyjamas.

'Oh, I was looking for you,' she said to Miss Eiseldown when she saw her.

'What's the matter, Amanda? It's only five o'clock.'

'I feel ill,' she groaned. Her teeth were chattering. Miss Eiseldown took off her dressing-gown and draped it around Amanda's shoulders.

'I think you may have measles,' the housemother said gently. 'Come down to sick-bay. I'll have to wake Matron.'

Emily couldn't believe her ears when Cassie woke her with the news at seven.

'Hey, you know what this means, don't you?' cried Emily excitedly.

'What?'

'You'll be dancing Red Riding Hood in the rehearsals while Amanda's ill.'

'Not if I've got to stay in my room, I won't,' said Cassie wearily.

'Oh, I'm sorry, Cassie, I'd forgotten!' said Emily.

'Anyway,' said Cassie, 'we've got more serious things to talk about.'

'You mean the ghost?'

'What else?'

'I'll bring Matthew and Tom here at first break,' said Emily.

'Well, be careful,' said Cassie.

True to her word, Emily brought the two boys to see Cassie at half past ten. She hadn't yet told them about the ghost.

'Come on then,' said Matthew. 'What's all the excitement? You do realise I'm giving up my iced bun for this.'

Tom and Matthew looked impressed when Emily had finished describing the nightmarish apparition of the previous night.

'And we're sure,' added Cassie, 'that it was the same figure we've seen before.'

'Do you think it's a real ghost then?' asked Matthew.

'Now we've had a good look at it, there isn't much doubt about it.'

'How do you mean?'

'Well, it was identical to the portrait of Petrakova – *exactly* the same costume.'

'It was dark,' said Tom.

'Not very,' said Cassie. 'There was a full moon last night. The white dress was easy to see. I've studied the pattern of tiny seed pearls sewn on to the *Giselle* bodice in the painting. It was just the same on the ghost's.'

Matthew whistled. 'So what's the ghost of Petrakova doing haunting your bedroom?'

'Not our bedroom,' said Cassie with a shiver of fear. 'Me! She was pointing at *me*!'

12

Ghost at the Window

Cassie was tired. Very, very tired. She was relieved when Emily, Tom and Matthew had to leave for their next lesson. She wondered if Miss Eiseldown would come to see her in the lunch-hour. Not feeling like facing any more visitors she quickly scrawled 'Do not disturb' on a piece of notepaper and stuck it outside her door. Then, with a great feeling of relief, she climbed back into bed. At last she could go to sleep now, without worrying about visitors – ghostly or otherwise.

As she lay there, her mind in a whirl, she remembered Becky with a pang. The ghost had driven thoughts about her friend out of her head.

Oh, if only Becky hadn't got sick in the first place. Despite what Miss Eiseldown had said, Cassie had serious doubts about Becky's recovery. But she had seemed so lively in the hospital. Could the illness really defeat Becky? Cassie hoped not, with all her heart and soul.

When Cassie woke again, she found her lunch tray standing on her desk and wondered how long she had been asleep. She was surprised to find that it was five o'clock. A few minutes later, Emily returned with her tea.

'You haven't touched your lunch!' she exclaimed.

'Only just got up,' said Cassie, yawning. She suddenly felt ravenously hungry and set about her tea with relish.

Emily yawned and collapsed on her bed. 'I think you've been in the best place today,' she said. 'Goodness, I'm shattered.'

'I bet,' said Cassie between mouthfuls. 'Any news?'

'Amanda has definitely got measles and is going to be out of action for a while.'

'Wonderful!' breathed Cassie.

'And everyone's talking about the ghost of course. Even the teachers were asking me about it.'

'Perhaps Miss Wrench will feel sorry for me and let me go back to lessons?' said Cassie.

'Mmm, perhaps,' said Emily doubtfully. She yawned again. 'Early to bed tonight. But there's masses of homework. You'd better do it too, or you'll have too much to catch up on.'

Strangely enough, Cassie didn't mind the idea of homework. She was refreshed by her afternoon nap and her mind needed something to occupy it. Better to think about homework than Petrakova's ghost!

She was deeply into an English essay when there was a knock on the door. It was a fifth year girl whom Cassie knew by sight.

'Which one of you's Cassandra Brown?' the girl asked.

'Me,' said Cassie.

'You're to come with me to Miss Wrench's office.'

'Right now?'

'Right now.'

Perhaps her hope was going to become a reality. She looked at Emily. Emily crossed her fingers and held them up.

Cassie followed the girl through the school. It felt rather strange to be out of her room again – rather like when you've been cooped up indoors for a week with an illness, and then you're allowed to go outside for the first time.

The fifth year knocked on Miss Wrench's door, but let Cassie go in alone. She was surprised to see Madame Larette standing beside the Wrench's desk. The Principal herself was seated.

Miss Wrench looked at her narrowly. 'We've heard reports of a ghost in your bedroom last night.'

'Yes, Miss Wrench. Emily and I both saw it.'

'And you're quite sure it looked like Anna Petrakova?'

'Quite sure. The pearl pattern on the bodice was identical.'

Madame Larette gasped. '*Mon Dieu!*' she cried. 'it *must* be 'er!'

'Now, now,' warned Miss Wrench. 'Please, Madame.'

But Madame Larette forged on, unquenched. 'We used to love 'er visits. She was full of grace – that's the only word for it. Grace. *Ma pauvre* Anna, so tragic for one so talented to be killed so young.'

'Can we get back to the subject of the ghost,' snapped Miss Wrench.

But Madame was not to be stopped, now she was in full flow. 'So young. Yes. Only two days after her thirty-third birthday. At the 'eight of 'er powers. The world at her feet – Russia, America, Canada, Japan. Oh, to think that—'

'Madame, that's enough!' ordered Miss Wrench, rising now to her feet. 'I want to conclude the interview with this student.'

Cassie's heart dived downwards, as she saw the cold expression on Miss Wrench's face.

'Now,' said Miss Wrench, when all was silent. 'Cassandra Brown, there is only one conclusion I can reach!' She paused. 'You are not only the thief who took Rebecca's silver charm, but also the thief who stole Petrakova's bronze slipper!'

'No!' Cassie burst out.

'I can't prove it . . . *yet*. But I *shall*. While I am getting to the root of the matter, you will be suspended from Redwood.'

'But Miss Wrench—' interrupted Madame Larette.

'What is it?'

'I cannot believe Cassandra is a thief. She must be innocent until proved guilty, *non*?'

'We can't have thieves – suspected thieves – at loose at Redwood,' answered Miss Wrench.

'But we don't even know what Rebecca will 'ave to say about the charm yet. And can you rely on the suspicions of a *phantom*?'

Miss Wrench hesitated and Madame took the opportunity to press on. 'And I *must* 'ave Cassandra this next two weeks, while Amanda is away with measles. She is 'er understudy, you remember? It would 'elp the continuity of rehearsals if Cassandra could dance the part – she knows it so well.'

The Principal drummed her fingers on the desk.

'Quite out of the question, Madame. No, Cassandra must be suspended from the weekend. I shall write to her parents immediately. In the meantime, Cassandra, you are to stay in your room.'

That evening, Cassie got permission from a sympathetic Miss Eiseldown to phone her parents, so that she could tell them about the suspension before Miss Wrench's letter arrived. She felt a strange mixture of longing and reluctance, when her mother answered the phone.

'Hello, Mum.'

'Oh, hello darling. I was just thinking about you. How are you?'

'Terrible.'

'Why, Cassie? What's wrong?'

Cassie gulped at the note of alarm in her mother's voice. Better come straight out with it.

'I've been suspended. Starting this weekend.'

There was a stunned silence at the other end. 'Suspended?'

'I've been accused of stealing, but it's not true, Mum. It's just not true.'

Cassie broke down and couldn't continue. Luckily Emily was at her elbow and took over the receiver. She told Joy Brown as much as she could, without giving the game away about the silver ballerina. When Cassie got back on the phone, her mother was over the initial shock and was able to give her daughter plenty of support and encouragement.

'We'll talk more at the weekend. It'll be lovely to have you home. And don't *worry* – we'll sort this out.'

Over the next couple of days, Cassie felt constantly tired and very low-spirited. Since her visit from the ghost, she had not had a good night's sleep. Longing for the weekend, when she could go home, she knew she would feel ten times better when she could share her troubles with her mum and dad.

She kept thinking about what she was missing, the preparations for the Gala above everything. She had been so thrilled about her solo and she had loved every minute of the Upper School rehearsals of *The Sleeping Beauty*. The Wedding

Act had begun to take shape and she had never tired of watching the other dancers – the dainty, delicate fairies, the amusing cats, the ethereal Bluebirds, the energetic Cossacks, but most of all Aurora and the Prince in their wonderful pas de deux.

Cassie was sitting on her bed, imagining herself dancing Aurora, when Emily came into her room, followed by Matthew and Tom.

'Hi,' said Matthew, dropping on to the bed beside her. 'Emily's told us about your suspension.'

'Yes, bad luck,' Tom chipped in.

'Can't you get an alibi sorted out?' asked Matthew.

'How do you mean?'

'For the night of the theft – who you were with and at what time. It could help a lot.'

Cassie sighed. 'I don't know. The Wrench just seems to have made up her mind it's me. And really, the ghost thing does make me look guilty, doesn't it?'

'It does a bit,' said Matthew.

'But I've been thinking a lot about it,' said Cassie, 'and I don't believe it was really Petrakova's ghost at all.'

'What?' exclaimed Emily.

'We didn't ever see her face, did we?' cried Cassie.

'No, but—'

'Well, there you are. Someone very carefully imitated the dress and deliberately set this whole thing up to frame me.'

'It's hard to believe,' said Emily, when she had taken in Cassie's meaning.

'Oh, I don't know. I find it harder to believe in ghosts, personally,' said Matthew.

'Me, too,' said Tom.

'*You* didn't see it!' said Emily, with a shudder.

'The unexpected is always frightening,' said Matthew wisely, 'especially when it's dark.'

'If I'm right,' said Cassie, 'I have to look for someone who wants to make me appear guilty, to hide their own guilt.'

'Right,' said Matthew. 'Then we're looking for the thief!'

'Trouble is, if I don't find out anything before the weekend . . .' She trailed off.

'Don't be silly, Cassie,' said Emily, 'We'll carry on the investigation for you. We'll find whoever it is.'

The remainder of the week proved uneventful. Emily was asked to understudy for Red Riding Hood and Jane took over Cassie's Nerine solo. Cassie felt very frustrated about this, but tried to keep herself in practice as much as she could in the small room, not forgetting ten minutes in her pointe shoes each day.

By the last night, she was in a terrible state. The thought kept nagging away at her that she might never come back to Redwood after this suspension.

'Oh, if only there was some good news about Becky!' she exclaimed to Emily, who was sitting on her bed, re-darning her pointe shoes.

'She's got to start feeling better soon,' said her friend. 'It's just a matter of time.'

'Yes, time I haven't got. We still haven't a clue whose the silver ballerina is, let alone who's been dressing up as the ghost.'

'Probably the same person,' said Emily.

'I'm sure you're right there!' cried Cassie. 'Oh, I'm so cooped up in here. I've got to get out and *do* something. Anything!'

'It's too dangerous,' Emily remonstrated.

'I can't be in any worse trouble than I'm in already,' argued Cassie. 'Come on, let's go out in the grounds. No one'll see us there.'

'Oh, all right, but I don't think it's a very good idea.'

It was still quite light, and very warm, when the two friends slipped out into the grounds. Cassie took in a lungful of fresh air and stretched her arms out wide.

'This is more like it. I'm feeling alive again!' she said.

'At least you'll be home tomorrow with your mum and dad,' said Emily. She sounded wistful.

'Do you still get homesick, Emily?'

'Yes, but not for home as it is now. What I miss is home as it used to be. Before Dad left us.'

'Do you still never see him?'

'No, we don't even know where he is. Oh, sorry, I'm trying to cheer you up, remember.'

'No, that's all right.' Cassie felt glad that Emily had been able to share something with her about

135

her father. She knew Emily found it terribly difficult to talk about him.

As they sauntered past the back of the building, they could see the windows of the rooms up on their landing. In one of them, the curtains had been drawn, and the light put on. Emily stopped and stared hard at the deep sash-window. 'Look!' she cried.

A shape was silhouetted against the curtains – a shape that they both knew they had seen before.

'It's the ghost, isn't it?' whispered Emily.

'It looks like it,' said Cassie, 'or else someone in a long ballet dress.'

'Let's go and see which room it is, shall we?' said Emily.

They rushed back into the building and had to hide round a corner when they saw their Geography teacher going past. When they reached their landing, they counted off the doors from the end wall.

'This one,' said Emily.

'Well, isn't that interesting?' Cassie said. 'Sharon and Sandra's room.'

They knocked on the door. There was a good deal of giggling and rustling before the door was opened by an innocent-looking Sandra. Sharon was standing over by the tape-recorder, choosing a tape. But there was no sign of anyone in a long ballet dress.

'Amanda's not here, is she?' asked Cassie.

'She's in sick-bay of course,' said Sandra.

There was no sign of any long ballet dress in the room. Cassie casually opened the wardrobe door and peeped inside. Nothing unusual.

'What do you think you're nosing at?' snapped Sharon.

'Was Amanda here a few minutes ago?' Cassie asked Sandra.

'No, she wasn't.'

'I thought *you* were supposed to stay in your room!' cried Sharon.

Cassie ignored her.

'You haven't seen anything . . . ?' asked Emily.

'Anything?' echoed Sandra.

'Well, anything funny, weird?'

'No,' she said, 'Why?'

'Oh, oh . . . nothing,' said Emily.

Sharon began to cough and Cassie suspected she was suppressing giggles.

'Well,' said Cassie, when she and Emily were back on the landing. 'What was so funny, I wonder?'

'Oh, those two are just daft. Why did you ask if Amanda had been in the room?'

'Oh, just a hunch.'

She's still ill isn't she?'

'Yes, but Matron can't watch her all the time. Particularly in the evenings.'

'Come to think of it, we'd better get you back in our room pretty quick, before one of the teachers sees you!'

'Oh, back to prison,' groaned Cassie. 'I suppose I'd better start packing.'

13

The Charm Bracelet

'I think I should go and get Matthew and Tom,' said Emily. 'We ought to tell them what we've just seen.'

'OK.' Cassie was feeling intensely miserable now she was back in her room and the thought of another meeting with the boys brightened up the prospect of an otherwise very dull evening.

When Emily returned with them, Matthew looked excited.

'It's got to be one of those two that's dressing up as the ghost!' he said, as soon as he'd got through the door.

'I'm not so sure,' said Cassie.

'Perhaps Sharon and Sandra just couldn't see what we could see from outside,' suggested Emily timidly.

'That's stupid!' cried Matthew. 'Cassie, I thought you'd decided it wasn't a real ghost.'

'I have,' said Cassie matter-of-factly. 'I just don't think it's Sharon or Sandra.'

'But why?'

'Firstly, I don't think they've got the brains to have copied that costume so well. Secondly, if they're involved, you can bet Amanda's at the root of it.'

'Even so,' said Tom, 'she'd have to be brilliant at needlework to make a costume like that.'

'Mmm,' said Cassie, 'I haven't worked that one out yet. But if she was in the room when we were outside, she could easily have hidden in the loo, or even under the bed.'

'What we need to do,' said Matthew, 'is to find the *Giselle* costume.'

Cassie looked thoughtful. 'How about having a good look round *this* room. I know the dress can't be here, but we were here when she collected her things, so if there was anything she didn't want us to see, she would have to have left it here.'

'Brilliant!' cried Matthew, admiringly.

Cassie blushed. 'When I was packing, I found Amanda's hanky on the floor – you know, Emily, that one we've noticed before.'

'Give it here,' said Matthew.

140

'Look at the initials,' said Cassie. 'Not A.R. but A.P.'

'Odd, isn't it,' agreed Matthew.

'Perhaps her middle name begins with P,' suggested Tom.

'Come on,' said Cassie. 'Let's have a good hunt round the room.'

'The cleaner doesn't do a very good job under these pieces of furniture, does she?' said Emily, scrabbling round on her hands and knees.

'What are we looking for?' asked Tom.

'Don't know till we find it,' said Matthew. He stretched his long arm beneath the wardrobe where the girls hung their coats and dresses and felt about with his fingers. 'You're right about the dust. Hang on, I've got something.'

He drew out a box of violin resin.

'Oh, I wondered where that had got to,' said Cassie. She was pulling out all the drawers from the chest which had held Amanda's belongings.

'Careful!' warned Emily. 'Don't upset my things.'

But Cassie turned over the bottom drawer, spilling the contents on to the floor.

'Cassie!' yelled Emily.

'Shh!' said Cassie.

Taped to the bottom drawer was a small parcel, wrapped in brown paper and sellotaped over and over many times. Excitedly, Cassie pulled it off and found a pair of scissors. She cut through the layers of wrappings.

'Look what we have here,' she crowed. She held

aloft, exultantly, a silver charm bracelet with one small empty ring to show where one of the charms had fallen off.

'That looks mighty suspicious for Amanda, doesn't it?'

Matthew whistled. 'Wish we could rush round to sick-bay and confront her with this!'

'No, you'll have to wait till she's back in circulation,' sighed Cassie. 'I'll miss all the fun!'

'Never mind,' said Matthew. 'We'll send you a postcard with a quote from Amanda.'

'So do you think Amanda's the thief?' asked Emily.

'It looks very much like it,' said Cassie.

'And she was quite prepared to let you take the blame,' said Emily. 'But why on earth should she want to steal a bronze ballet shoe?'

Cassie shrugged. 'Perhaps she'll tell all when you wave the charm bracelet under her nose.'

'Come on Matthew,' said Tom. 'We'd better go. It's getting late.'

'OK,' said Matthew reluctantly. 'Meet us tomorrow at breakfast, Emily. We still need to find that *Giselle* dress.'

He turned to Cassie. 'Bye, Casablanca. I'm sure you won't be away long. Wish us luck with the investigation.'

Cassie snorted. 'I've cracked it for you,' she said. 'You've only got the ends to tie up.'

Matthew grinned. 'There seem to be plenty of those. See you.'

It was almost bedtime. Cassie put the finishing touches to her packing and had just changed into her pyjamas when there was a knock on the door.

'Oh, no,' groaned Emily, 'not the boys back again surely.'

But when Cassie opened the door, she had a shock. It was her dad!

'Mum said you were picking me up on Saturday morning!' she exclaimed.

'Aren't you pleased to see me?' said Jake.

'Of course I am.'

She gave him a hug. 'Well, at least I'm packed. But I'll have to get out of my pyjamas.'

Jake looked rather flushed. 'I've just been to see Miss Wrench,' he said.

'You haven't, have you?' cried Cassie in surprise.

'Yes, and I gave her a piece of my mind about the way she's been treating you!'

'Oh, Dad, I bet you've made it worse! I know what your temper's like.'

Jake grinned. 'No, I've made it distinctly better. She's lifted the suspension.'

'What!' yelled Cassie, jumping up and throwing her arms around him. 'Oh, you lovely Dad, you! How did you do it?'

'Well, we've been in contact with Mr and Mrs Hastings, and as soon as Becky began to feel better, they let me go down to see her. She told me the *whole* story about the silver ballerina.' He stopped and looked intently at his daughter. Cassie felt a bit uncomfortable – she wished she had told her parents the whole truth – but more than anything she felt delighted.

'Oh, I'm so pleased Becky's getting better again,' she said.

'Anyway,' continued Jake, 'it wasn't an easy interview with Miss Wrench. She seemed to have made up her mind that you're guilty and at first she wouldn't believe Becky's story at all.'

'How did you convince her, Dad?'

Jake smiled. 'I was prepared. I'd made a tape-recording of Becky, as she still can't write.'

'So does she think I'm innocent now?' asked Cassie hopefully.

'Well, I don't know, to be quite frank. She really seems to have a bee in her bonnet about you. But the fact is that she has no evidence, therefore it would be quite unjust to punish you further. I said I would complain to the Trustees if she did.'

'Oh, Dad, you're great!' said Cassie, hugging him again.

'So it's lessons as usual on Monday,' said Jake. 'Pop your clothes back on. I'm taking you home for the weekend.'

Cassie didn't argue. The relief of having her parents' support was so intense that she knew a weekend at home was just what she needed to recharge her batteries. When she was ready, she said goodbye to a rather wistful-looking Emily.

'And good luck with the search,' she whispered.

'More secrets?' asked Jake, raising his bushy eyebrows.

'Nothing to worry about, Dad!' Cassie said laughing, and followed her dad to his car.

On Sunday evening, Cassie flew into her room with her suitcase and violin and shut the door firmly behind her.

'Did you find anything out?' she asked breathlessly.

'Not a thing,' said Emily.

'Come on, let's go and see Matthew and Tom! We've got to sort this out!'

So they made their way, watchfully, to the boys' block. They met only one teacher on the way and that, by good fortune, was Madame Larette, who never concerned herself with school rules.

Safely inside Matthew's room, Cassie described her father's interview with Miss Wrench.

'I'd love to have been a fly on the wall,' remarked Matthew. 'You're jolly lucky to have a headmaster for a father, Cassie.'

'I didn't think so when I went to his school,' laughed Cassie.

'We're still no nearer solving the mystery of the ghost though,' said Matthew as though it were needling him.

'It must have been Amanda!' cried Cassie.

'Well if it was,' Matthew replied, 'you won't be seeing spooks again for another week or so!'

'Right. Watch her carefully, when she gets back,' said Tom.

'That's all we can do, really,' said Cassie. 'And

show her the bracelet, of course.'

'Yes, I think we should forget all about it till then,' said Emily.

Taking her friend's advice, Cassie put the mystery to the back of her mind. It was lovely to take part in lessons again. She had really missed her dancing classes, and, although she had practised in her room, it took her a few days to get back into top condition. Of course there were extra rehearsals too. The Juniors' underwater ballet was shaping up very well, and Madame Larette was still working her and Emily very hard on their nymph solos.

Cassie felt bad about taking over the understudying of Red Riding Hood from Emily, but her friend insisted she didn't mind in the least.

'I've enjoyed the rehearsals I've been involved in,' she said. 'It was a super experience, but after all you've been through, you deserve a chance to dance the part.'

'You're a great friend, Em,' said Cassie. 'I suppose it is only for a few more days, anyway, before Amanda claims it back.'

'Yes, worse luck!' said Emily.

'I'm going to make the most of it till then!' Cassie said. 'Do you fancy coming across to Mrs Allingham's with me this lunch-hour?'

'Any particular reason?'

'Well, partly to see her, and, yes, I've a question to ask her.'

She would tell Emily no more until they had arrived at Mrs Allingham's cottage and done some cleaning for her. Then, over a glass of lemonade, Cassie brought the conversation round to Anna Petrakova.

'You really are interested in Anna, aren't you, Cassandra,' the old lady laughed. 'But I can understand it. She is a most tragic, romantic figure.'

'I'd love to have seen her dance,' said Emily.

'Yes, it was a rare experience,' said Mrs Allingham. 'Now, what was it you wanted to know, Cassandra?'

'Well, you know you told us about her death? From blood-poisoning, I think you said?'

'Yes?'

'You didn't tell us how she came to get the blood-poisoning, did you?'

'No, I didn't, did I?' said Mrs Allingham, with a rather secretive smile. 'By the way,' she said, changing the subject, 'I hear you've been in some trouble with Miss Wrench, Cassandra.'

Despite her innocence, Cassie immediately turned bright red. 'Did she tell you about it?' she asked.

'Yes, she mentioned it a couple of days ago. Thankfully, by then, your father had already sorted things out, otherwise I would have put in a good word for you.'

'Thanks, Mrs Allingham.'

'You must tread carefully, Cassandra. Miss Wrench is not a good enemy to have. She is in the most powerful position at Redwood. Never forget that!'

'I won't,' said Cassie. 'But you didn't answer my question, about Petrakova.'

Mrs Allingham sighed. 'The young never forget, do they?'

Cassie and Emily laughed.

'Well, I don't suppose it'll hurt if I tell you. But it is not meant to be common knowledge, you do understand?'

'Yes, Mrs Allingham!' chorused the girls.

'Anna Petrakova died of blood-poisoning, after giving birth to a child.'

Emily was amazed to find that Cassie didn't look the least surprised.

'Was the child a girl?' Cassie asked.

'Yes, I believe she was, dear.'

Cassie remembered Mrs Allingham's warning about Miss Wrench when the day came that she took *The Sleeping Beauty* rehearsal. Cassie had butterflies in her tummy as soon as she saw her there in the studio, tapping her stick and looking irritable. The fairies' dances at the beginning went very well, luckily, and the Wrench seemed better-humoured by the time the Cats began their dance. The girl playing Puss-in-Boots looked terribly nervous, Cassie thought. During the sequence, she suddenly and completely forgot her steps and just stood still, as though in a dream. Miss Wrench was furious, and even though the following Bluebird pas de deux was excellent, she stayed in a snappy mood and didn't offer them a word of praise. Cassie felt her legs trembling as she waited for the music which signalled Red Riding Hood's entrance. She was so glad that there were no difficult steps for her to do – she was sure she would have come unstuck. As it was, she got through the dance, and so did Matthew, but without their usual sparkle.

Miss Wrench took the opportunity to vent her spite on Cassie, in front of all the other students.

'Heaven knows why Madame made such a fuss about your taking part in these rehearsals. Any one of your class would have made a better job of the part than you! Thank goodness Amanda will be back next week.'

For the rest of the rehearsal, Cassie had to fight back her anger. Miss Wrench's cutting words had brought her face to face with the harsh truth that the Principal almost certainly still believed Cassie to be the thief who had taken Petrakova's slipper.

14

End of the Hunt

'Have you seen her?' Emily asked Cassie over breakfast one morning the following week.

'Who?' asked Cassie, absent-mindedly shovelling muesli into her mouth.

'Amanda, of course! Look, she's over there with you-know-who.'

Sure enough, Amanda was out of sick-bay and sitting with Sharon and Sandra. Cassie felt a surge of excitement.

'Let's write her a note, asking her to meet us in our room.'

'What then?'

'We'll get the boys to come too. And then we'll

show her the bracelet. We might get a confession out of her.'

'Do you think so?' asked Emily, doubtfully.

'If we play it right, yes, I think we will.'

Emily didn't share her friend's confidence, knowing how self-possessed Amanda normally was.

The note was written later:

Dear Amanda,
Meet us in our room at one thirty. We have something of yours which you may want back.
Cassie and Emily.

The girls posted it under Amanda's door and scurried off to ballet class, to face Miss Oakland's critical eye. Cassie hadn't been in trouble with the young ballet mistress for some time, but this morning her mind wouldn't stay on ballet. Miss Oakland quickly noticed Cassie's lack of concentration.

'I thought we'd got over that silly stage, Cassandra,' she bellowed. 'Your feet are useless without a bit of brainpower attached.'

'Sorry, Miss Oakland,' Cassie said sheepishly.

'Don't let it happen again,' warned the teacher.

Cassie wondered how much Miss Wrench had told the other staff. It was horrible to feel that the teachers might not trust her. She wondered what her chances were of staying at Redwood for all that much longer. Unless of course, Amanda confessed to the theft!

Unfortunately, this speculation sparked off another train of thought about the lunch-time meeting with Amanda. Miss Oakland stopped the class in the middle of a ronde de jambe en l'air.

'Cassandra!' she said, with an edge to her voice. 'It's quite clear to me that you are not with us this morning. Therefore I suggest you take your body where your mind is!'

As graciously as she could, Cassie curtsied and walked out, head held high, chin jutting slightly forward.

'Miss Oakland was in a bad mood for the rest of the lesson,' said Emily at lunch-time.

Cassie looked at her watch. 'Amanda should be here in a minute.'

There was a tap on the door. Cassie let Matthew and Tom in.

'I'm glad you've got here before Amanda,' she said.

'If she comes,' said Emily.

'She'll come,' said Cassie.

A couple of minutes later, Amanda barged in without knocking.

'What have you got of mine?' she demanded, without ceremony.

'All in good time, Amanda,' said Cassie. 'We wondered if you'd noticed anything missing?'

'Missing?' she said. 'Nothing, apart from your brains.'

'Oh, *very* funny,' Cassie retorted. 'Tried on any long ballet dresses lately?'

'What *is* this, an interrogation?' she snapped. 'Just give me what's mine. I've got things to do.'

'Hold on a minute,' said Cassie. 'We want a few questions answered first.'

'I'm not staying here another moment!' Amanda declared, walking towards the door. Cassie intercepted her. She had a brown paper parcel in her hand, sellotaped over and over.

'Recognise it?' she said, holding it out towards Amanda.

'Yes, it's mine,' said Amanda, trying to snatch it.

'Manners!' said Cassie, holding the parcel out of Amanda's reach.

'Give it to me!' she yelled.

'Would you like to see what's inside?' Matthew asked.

'No,' she said, 'I know what's inside. And you'd better not have opened it!'

'Well, just in case you've forgotten,' said Cassie, diving off to get the scissors and open the parcel, 'let's all have a look, shall we?'

'How dare you!' shouted Amanda. She looked furious.

Cassie tore open the package and held up the silver charm bracelet. 'See, here's where the little ballerina fits. How come it was dropped so near the display case, Amanda?'

Amanda had gone very pale. 'I don't know what you're talking about,' she said.

'And why didn't you tell the Wrench it was yours?' cried Emily.

Amanda laughed. 'Use your brains!'

'You nearly got Cassie expelled!' Emily yelled.

'Oh, *what* a shame!' said Amanda.

'It was you who stole the bronze ballet shoe, wasn't it?' said Cassie firmly.

'Don't be *stupid*!' cried Amanda. 'Why should I want to steal my—'

She clamped her mouth shut as though horrified by what she had nearly let slip and sat down heavily on the bed. Cassie could see that she was on the verge of bursting into tears and curiously stopped feeling angry with her. There was a few moments' silence; then Matthew snapped his fingers. 'I get it!' he shouted. 'A.P.!'

'Spell it out Matthew,' said Tom.

'I thought I just had,' said Matthew. 'A.P. – Anna Petrakova!'

'But what's Amanda doing with Petrakova's hanky?' asked Emily.

'Come on, you two twits!' said Cassie impatiently. 'Surely, it's obvious. Amanda is Anna Petrakova's daughter. Aren't you, Amanda?'

Amanda made no reply.

'Is it really true?' asked Emily.

'Of course it is!' answered Cassie. 'Mrs Allingham told us Anna had a daughter before she died. We've never seen Amanda's mother. And it explains why the Wrench thinks Amanda's Number One. She's probably the only one at

Redwood who knows who Amanda really is.'

'But surely that clears her of stealing the slipper,' said Emily, looking confused. 'She'd hardly steal her own mother's memento.'

Funny noises started coming from Amanda's direction. Cassie looked round at her and saw that she was laughing and crying at the same time.

'Oh, you always were thick, Emily,' Amanda said, in a strangled voice. 'How do you think it feels being the daughter of a famous ballerina with your dad always expecting you to have the same success? Expecting you to be another Anna Petrakova?'

The four friends were silent in the face of Amanda's strong emotions.

'I hate her, do you know that? I can't just be me, I've got to be *her*!'

'But why did you take her ballet shoe?' asked Cassie.

'I don't know,' said Amanda. 'I had it all planned way back. I just knew I wanted to destroy that display.'

Her voice choked with sobs. Emily sat down beside her and put an arm round her. Matthew raised his eyes heavenwards in disgust.

'How did you open the case?' he asked, after Amanda had quietened down again.

'Easy – Dad has a set of all the keys. He's the chief trustee of Redwood.'

'And where did the dress come from?' Cassie demanded.

'My mother's wardrobe at home – it's full of her

old ballet costumes. I smuggled it into school.'

'So you *were* the ghost!' shrieked Emily, jumping up. 'You nearly frightened the life out of us.'

Amanda started laughing again – laughter mixed with sobs. 'That was the idea. But then it came to me that it was the perfect way to pin the theft on someone else, and get rid of Cassie at the same time.'

'But why?' exclaimed Emily.

'Because I've got to be the best,' sobbed Amanda. 'I've got to be!'

'But I thought you said you didn't want to follow in your mother's footsteps,' said Cassie, confused. 'Why should you mind that I'm as good as you at dancing?'

'It doesn't matter whether *you* succeed or not,' yelled Amanda in reply. '*Your* parents will love you, whatever you do. I've *got* to be the best!'

She broke down into bitter crying and refused to say any more.

The others felt uncomfortable and went out of the room on to the landing.

'I think we should go and find Miss Eiseldown,' said Cassie.

'Good idea,' said Matthew, 'and Tom and I will go and see Miss Wrench, with the bracelet. She'll take it better from us than you.'

On their way to Miss Eiseldown's room, a thought struck Emily which made her shout out loud.

'The itching powder!'

Cassie grinned at her. 'I'm three steps ahead of

you,' she said. 'As soon as she mentioned her father's keys, I knew. She could easily unlock Madame's cupboard.'

The girls soon found Miss Eiseldown, and tried to explain to her what had been happening.

'Oh, don't gabble at the same time!' she pleaded. She made them sit down with her in her room, and asked Emily to tell the story.

'You see, Miss Eiseldown,' said Emily, 'it was Amanda who took the bronze ballet shoe, and Amanda who dressed herself up as Petrakova's ghost, to make Cassie look guilty.'

'Thank you, Emily, that was nice and clear. The only problem I have is why? And how?'

'Amanda is Anna Petrakova's daughter,' said Cassie.

'Petrakova's daughter! Good heavens! I didn't even know she had one!'

'Amanda's dad wants Amanda to be a great ballerina like Anna. Only I think Amanda's sort of cracking up under the pressure,' said Emily.

'And that's why we want you to come with us,' urged Cassie, 'because Amanda's hysterical, now she knows we know.'

'Oh, yes,' said Miss Eiseldown, getting up hurriedly, 'I'll go to her straight away.'

When they reached the bedroom, they found Miss Wrench telling Matthew and Tom they were no longer needed. Amanda was still sobbing on the bed, so Miss Eiseldown took it upon herself to comfort her.

Miss Wrench looked up at Cassie and Emily. 'Come and help me search Amanda's room, you two girls,' she said. 'You know what we're looking for – and unless we find the dress or the ballet shoe, take it from me, I won't believe a word of your story.'

Despite what she said, Cassie could tell from Miss Wrench's tone that she already more than half-believed it. It must be hard for her, she thought, to accept that her favourite pupil had done such awful things.

They made their way to Sharon and Sandra's room, Miss Eiseldown guiding Amanda along behind. The room was unoccupied. Miss Wrench, Cassie and Emily searched through every chest of drawers, every desk and locker and the wardrobe, but there was no sign of either item.

'Well?' Miss Wrench demanded. The girls looked at one another helplessly.

'Perhaps we should ask Amanda?' said Miss Eiseldown quietly.

Everyone had forgotten she was even in the room. Miss Wrench looked surprised.

'I can try, I suppose. Amanda dear,' she began in the sugary voice she always reserved for Amanda, 'do you know anything about a *Giselle* costume? I mean, have you brought one here, to school?'

Amanda sat up, her previous pallor having given way to a swollen redness. 'What if I did. It's *mine* now.'

'And where is it, Amanda?' asked Miss Wrench,

her tone tightening. 'And more importantly, *where* is your mother's bronze ballet slipper?'

No one could withstand that steely stare, not even Amanda.

'In the toilet cistern,' was the sullen reply.

'Good Lord!' cried Miss Wrench, horrified. 'Cassandra,' she commanded, 'search that . . . that *receptacle*, if you would.'

Cassie disappeared into the loo and returned with a dripping bundle of frothy net and something the shape and size of a ballet shoe, wrapped in a black bin liner.

'Here you are, Miss Wrench,' she said, offering the articles to her.

'I don't want them!' she snapped. 'Emily, find a bag or something.'

Emily quickly found a carrier, and the dress which had caused Cassie so much fright and trouble was stuffed into a polythene bag with a picture of Mickey Mouse on the front.

'I suppose we had better check the contents of this bag,' said Miss Wrench, turning to the black bin liner. 'Cassandra, would you . . . ?'

Cassie dutifully unwrapped the bin liner and revealed the gleaming bronze slipper.

'Well!' exclaimed Miss Wrench, sitting down on Amanda's bed. For once, she seemed lost for words.

'Shall I go and telephone Amanda's father?' asked Miss Eiseldown timidly.

'Yes,' said Miss Wrench. 'Good idea.'

'Emily, would you go and fetch Matron up here

please,' said Miss Eiseldown, more confidently. 'And ask her to phone for the doctor too.'

Miss Wrench sat dumbly on the bed, as though she were a stuffed animal.

Amanda had stopped crying and, once the door had closed on the others, the room became unbearably quiet. Cassie sat next to her old rival and just quietly held her hand, waiting for Emily to come back with Matron.

Miss Wrench turned to her suddenly, breaking the silence. 'Cassandra,' she said in a very husky voice, 'I'm sorry.'

With her innocence proved, a great weight was lifted from Cassie's shoulders. But, over the next few weeks, she thought about Amanda a great deal. Of course, she couldn't help feeling glad she was gone, but now she understood the sort of pressure Amanda had been under, she felt sorry for her too.

Amanda had broken under the pressure to succeed. Cassie vowed never to let that happen to her, despite her intense ambition to become a dancer.

At last came the day everyone had been waiting for – the end-of-year Gala. Cassie and Emily sat side by side on the coach which was to take them to the city's Repertory theatre where their production was to be staged. They were to arrive for a dress rehearsal at ten o'clock.

Miss Eiseldown called out the names on her

register and discovered Matthew was missing. She sent Tom to try and find him.

'Just like Matthew,' giggled Emily. Just as Tom disappeared into the school, Matthew came running out of another entrance. Everyone on the coach laughed. Except Miss Eiseldown. She sent Matthew straight back to find Tom.

'This could go on for hours,' laughed Cassie. Luckily though, it didn't, and they were soon spilling out of the coach, laden with suitcases and props and folded backdrops.

It was the first time Emily and Cassie had been inside the Rep. and so, once they had put their costumes in one of the dressing-rooms, they had a look round. It was very exciting to explore backstage. They were called quite quickly for rehearsal, however, as the Juniors' underwater ballet was first on the programme. After changing into their nymph tunics, they went up on stage, where Madame Larette was positioning her dancers. The bright lights on the stage, contrasting with the deep blackness of the auditorium, immediately made Cassie feel nervous. She imagined hundreds of people sitting out there, watching her.

It took a while for her class to get the hang of the stage – it was very different from dancing their ballet in the studio. For a start, the stage sloped gently, and of course the proportions were not the same. There wasn't much time to rehearse. All too soon, it was the second years' turn, and Emily and Cassie had a long break.

They met up with Matthew and Tom.

'Well,' said Matthew, 'last day of our first year. Can you believe it?'

'Not really,' said Cassie. 'I bet we'll all feel really flat and bored tomorrow at home.'

'Yes, there's been so much excitement lately,' said Emily.

'Too much excitement for my liking!' added Cassie. 'But just think, no Amanda next term to bother us!'

'Have you heard how she is?' asked Tom.

'Yes,' said Cassie. 'Miss Eiseldown told us yesterday that Amanda has had a breakdown. She's having counselling.'

'Perhaps now her dad has accepted she's not going to be a carbon copy of her mother,' said Emily.

'And her doctor has said it's unwise for her to continue with ballet training – at least until she's sorted herself out.'

'That doesn't mean she might come back?' asked Matthew.

'No,' answered Cassie. 'Miss Eiseldown seemed to think she'd never come back to Redwood.'

'No more mysteries, thank goodness,' said Emily.

Rehearsals were finished in time for the cast to have their packed lunches early, in their dressing-rooms. Cassie felt like a real performer as she sat there, dabbing on greasepaint, glancing in the mirror surrounded by lights, and tucking into a bag of crisps.

163

They had only just finished their make-up when Miss Eiseldown put her head round the door and smiled at them. 'Opening number,' she called.

The first years trooped out into the wings, waiting for the overture coming over the loudspeakers, to finish. Cassie could just glimpse a few faces in the front row but sensed a packed theatre. She wondered where her own family were sitting, and began to feel butterflies in her stomach. As soon as she set foot on stage, they disappeared. She forgot about the audience completely and danced as if in a dream. By the time she was dancing her solo, Cassie felt she had become the nymph Nerine, and was actually startled by the applause which she and Emily received for their dance. It was only later she discovered how loud and long the applause had been.

Sitting back in the dressing-room, while the other years presented their ballets, Cassie couldn't quite believe that everything had turned out so well for her in the end. At the show's finish, parents came streaming backstage to pick up their sons and daughters. Before Emily left with her mother, Cassie gave her a big hug.

'See you next term, Em,' she said. 'Say goodbye to our room for me.' Cassie already had all her belongings with her in the dressing-room, to save her own parents having to call at Redwood on their way home later that evening.

'Bye, Cassie, I'll write.' As she waved Emily off

from her dressing-room, her own mum and dad appeared.

'You were wonderful, Cassie,' said Joy, giving her a big hug. Then it was her dad's turn. He gave her a box of chocolate peppermints – her favourite.

'Wow!' said Matthew, popping his head round the door. 'Looks like I've arrived at the right time.'

'This is Matthew,' said Cassie, 'alias the Wolf.'

'Are your parents taking you out to tea?' asked Joy.

'No – they couldn't make the matinée. I don't think they could stand seeing their only son dressed up as an octopus.'

The Browns laughed.

'But they're coming to watch me doing my werewolf bit tonight!'

'Well, you must join us,' said Joy. 'You'll be bored stiff here on your own.'

'Thank you,' said Matthew gratefully. Cassie smiled, but she didn't much like the way he was looking at her chocolate peppermints.

'Where are Rachel and Adam, by the way?' she asked.

'We left them in the foyer,' said her dad. 'Ready?'

When they entered the foyer, Cassie couldn't believe her eyes! Becky was standing there with her brother and sister.

'Oh, Becky,' she yelled, running over and hugging her, 'I didn't know you were here – what a brilliant surprise!'

'It was *meant* to be a surprise!' said Becky,

grinning. 'Can we go and have tea now? I'm starving.'

'That sounds like the old Becky,' laughed Cassie. 'Oh, you look great. When did you get out of hospital?'

'Last week. I'm not wasting any time. I've learned to ride my bike again and I even managed to stand on one leg yesterday!'

'I can see we'll have you back at ballet school yet!' said Cassie.

'Well, I don't know about that,' said Becky.

After a filling tea of pasta, downed in a nearby Italian restaurant, Cassie wondered if she'd manage to dance at all in the evening performance. But when the time came, she and Matthew danced their pas de deux of Red Riding Hood and the Wolf as though they had been doing it all their lives.

After the ballet, Cassie felt as though she were floating; Becky was coming to stay with her for the first week of the holidays, her name had been cleared, and here she was, taking part in a real full-length classical ballet in a real theatre. It was the happiest day of her life.

THE BALLET SCHOOL, MAL LEWIS JONES

60729 7	CASSIE AT THE BALLET SCHOOL	£2.99
60731 9	NEW FRIENDS AT THE BALLET SCHOOL	£2.99
60732 7	TROUBLE AT THE BALLET SCHOOL	£2.99

THE MYSTERY CLUB, FIONA KELLY

58867 5	SECRET CLUES	£2.99
58868 3	DOUBLE DANGER	£2.99
58869 1	FORBIDDEN ISLAND	£2.99
58870 5	MISCHIEF AT MIDNIGHT	£2.99
59283 4	DANGEROUS TRICKS	£2.99
59284 2	MISSING!	£2.99
60723 8	HIDE AND SEEK	£3.50

All these books are available at your local bookshop or newsagent or can be ordered direct from the publisher. Just tick the titles you want and fill in the form below.

Prices and availability subject to change without notice.

HODDER AND STOUGHTON PAPERBACKS, PO BOX 11, Falmouth, Cornwall. Please send cheque or postal order for the value of the book, and add the following for postage and packing.

UK including BFPO – £1.00 for one book, plus 50p for the second book, and 30p for each additional book ordered up to a £3.00 maximum.

OVERSEAS including EIRE – £2.00 for the first book, plus £1.00 for the second book, and 50p for each additional book ordered.

OR Please debit this amount from my Access/Visa Card (delete as appropriate).

Card Number

Amount: £ ....

Expiry Date   ....

Signed   ....

Name   ....

Address   ....

....

....